Karl Elze

Notes on Elizabethan Dramatists

Karl Elze

Notes on Elizabethan Dramatists

ISBN/EAN: 9783337377007

Printed in Europe, USA, Canada, Australia, Japan

Cover: Foto ©Andreas Hilbeck / pixelio.de

More available books at **www.hansebooks.com**

NOTES ON ELIZABETHAN DRAMATISTS

WITH

CONJECTURAL EMENDATIONS OF THE TEXT.

BY

KARL ELZE,
PH. D., LL. D., HON. M.R.S.L.

THIRD SERIES.

HALLE:
MAX NIEMEYER.
1886.

As the following pages treat largely of that kind of verse, which, for want of a better name, I have designated as syllable pause lines, I think it right to inform the reader that some time ago (in October 1885), in turning over George L. Craik's edition of 'Julius Cæsar' (The English of Shakespeare &c., 5ᵗʰ Ed., Lon., 1875), I lighted accidentally at .p. 33 on a passage, hitherto overlooked by me, that bears upon this kind of apparently defective lines, which lines, Mr Craik says, appear to have received the sanction of Coleridge, in so far as Coleridge considered the pause a substitute for the omitted syllable. Craik, for his own part, confesses himself strongly inclined to think the text corrupted in all, or almost all, such cases; Coleridge, he says, had not fully considered the matter. I do not know, where Coleridge has treated of syllable pause lines and can do no more than refer the reader to the passage in Craik, without adding any comment of my own. My conviction is rather strengthened than shaken by Craik's remarks and I have continued to point out at least part of those lines in which a pause does service for a defective syllable.

As to the conjectural emendations on Marston's 'Insatiate Countess' (Nos CCCXXXIV— CCCXL), it should be .

distinctly understood that they were made without any other literary help than that afforded by Mr J. O. Halliwell's edition; I am sorry to say that it was out of my power to collate the quarto of 1613 of that play, which, in note CCLXXIII, I have shown to be far more correctly printed than the one made use of by Mr Halliwell.

For the rest, the Third (and probably last) Series of these Notes, like its two predecessors, must try to make its way on either side of the 'silver sea', which, I hope, will not 'serve in the office of a wall' against contributions towards the revision and elucidation of the text of the 'Sweet Swan of Avon', from whatever part of the world they may come.

Halle, March 13, 1886.   K. E.

CONTENTS.

CCCXVI.

Too often interviews amongst women, as amongst princes,
breed envy oft to other's fortune.

DEKKER AND WEBSTER, WESTWARD HO, I, 2
(WEBSTER, ED. DYCE, 1857, IN I VOL., 213b).

In The Dramatic Works of Thomas Dekker &c. (London,
1873), where Westward Ho! has been printed from the Quarto
of 1607, this passage stands thus (II, 291): too often inter-
viewes amongst women, as amongst Princes, breeds enuy oft
to others fortune. — *Oft*, after *too often*, can hardly be right;
qy. *of one*? The passage would then read: Too often interviews amongst women, as amongst princes, breed envy *of one*
to other's fortune.

CCCXVII.

I heard say that he would have had thee nursed thy child
thyself too.

IB., I, 2 (WEBSTER, ED. DYCE, 214a).

In The Dramatic Works of Thomas Dekker (Lon. 1873)
II, 292, the passage reads: I heard say that he would haue
had thee nurst thy Childe thy selfe too. — *Nursed*, or *nurst*,
is to all appearance a mere misprint for *nurse*.

CCCXVIII.

Mist. Honey[*suckle*]. I think, when all's done, I must
follow his counsel, and take a patch; I['d] have had one

I

long ere this, but for disfiguring my face: yet I had noted that a mastic patch upon some women's temples hath been the very rheum [rheuwme, Dekker, Dram. Works, II, 298] of beauty.

IB., II, 1 (WEBSTER, ED. DYCE, 216a).

Dyce remarks on the word *rheum*: 'A misprint, I believe: but qy. for what?' I think for *prime*. Another corruption seems still to be lurking in the passage; may not the original reading have been: yet I *have* noted?

───

CCCXIX.

Such a red lip, such a white forehead, such a black eye, such a full cheek, and such a goodly little nose, now she's in that French gown, Scotch falls, Scotch bum, and Italian head-tire you sent her, and is such an enticing she-witch, carrying the charms of your jewels about her.

IB., II, 2 (WEBSTER, ED. DYCE, 218b).

'Scotch falls, Scotch bum' is an evident dittography. Read either DUTCH *falls*, *Scotch bum*, or, *Scotch falls*, DUTCH *bum*. It may be left to the antiquaries to inquire which of these two conjectural emendations is countenanced by the Dutch and Scotch fashions of the time. — In Dekker's Dramatic Works, II, 302, the passage is given without the least alteration, except in the spelling.

───

CCCXX.

Whirl [*pool*]. We'll take a coach and ride to Ham or so.

Mist. Ten [*terhook*]. O, fie upon 't, a coach! I cannot abide to be jolted.

Mist. Wafer. Yet most of your citizens' wives love jolting.

IB., II, 3 (WEBSTER, ED. DYCE, 222b).

The last speech comes very inappropriately from Mistress Wafer's lips, she being a citizen's wife herself. In my judgment it should be assigned to one of the three gentlemen, Linstock, Whirlpool, and Sir Gosling Glowworm, most probably to Mr Whirlpool, as it is he who has made the proposal of taking a coach. — In The Dramatic Works of Thomas Dekker &c. (Lon. 1873), II, 311, the prefixes to these three speeches are: *While*; *Tent.* [i. e. *Mist. Tenterhook*]; and Mab[ell].

GREENE.

CCCXXI.

I have struck him dumb, my-lord; and, if your honour please.
> FRIAR BACON AND FRIAR BUNGAY, VI, 162 (THE DRAMATIC AND POETICAL WORKS OF ROB. GREENE AND GEORGE PEELE, ED. DYCE, 1861, IN I VOL., 162 b).

Dyce rather boldly suggests: *if you please* instead of *if your honour please*, whereas the late Professor Wilhelm Wagner in Professor Wülker's Anglia, II, 524, declares the line to be an Alexandrine. In my opinion it is a regular blankverse with an extra syllable before the pause; read and scan: —

I've struck | him dumb, | m'lord; and if | your hon|our
please.

CCCXXII.

I have given non-plus to the Paduans,
To them of Sien, Florence, and Bologna,
Rheims, Louvain, and fair Rotterdam,
Frankfort, Utrecht, and Orleans.
> IB., IX, 111 SEQ. (GREENE AND PEELE, ED. DYCE, 168 a).

'This [viz. the last] line, says Dyce, is certainly mutilated; and so perhaps is the preceding line: from the Emperor's

1*

speech, p. 159, first col., it would seem that "Paris" ought to be one of the places mentioned here.' — Dyce is quite right, but the mere addition of 'Paris' is no sufficient cure of the two defective lines. I strongly suspect that Greene wrote : —

I have given non-plus to the Paduans,
To them of Sien, Florence, and Bologna,·
Of Rheims, *of* Louvain, and fair Rotterdam,
Of Frankfort, Utrecht, *Paris* and Orleans.

The last line has an extra syllable before the pause and a trochee after it; scan therefore: —

Of Frank|fort, U|trecht, Páris | and Or|leáns.

──────

CCCXXIII.

All hail to this royal company.
IB., IX, 117 (GREENE AND PEELE, ED. DYCE, 168a).

According to Prof. Wagner (l. c.) this is an unmetrical line which he corrects by the insertion of *right* before *royal*. Prof. Ward (Old English Drama, ed. A. W. Ward, Oxford, 1878, 83) proposes to read *unto* instead of *to*. To me the line seems to be quite correct, if considered as a syllable pause line; scan: —

All hail! | ∪ to | this roy|al ‚com|pany.

──────

CCCXXIV.

Gracious as the morning-star of heaven.
IB., IX, 174 (GREENE AND PEELE, ED. DYCE, 168b).

In Prof. Wagner's eyes (l. c.) this is a remarkable instance of the conservative tendency of the editors; he does not hesitate to declare in favour of Prof. Ward's conjectural emendation (Old English Drama, 249):—

Gracious as *is* the morning-star of heaven.

But may not the poet have used *Gracious* as a trisyllable:—

Graci|ous as | the mor|ning-star | of heaven?

Or it may be a syllable pause line, as there is certainly a pause after *Gracious*:—

Gracious | ◡ as | the mor|ning-star | of heaven.

CCCXXV.

And give us cates fit for country swains.

Ib., IX, 240 (Greene and Peele, ed. Dyce, 169b).

Professor Wagner (l. c. 525) needlessly inserts *but* after *fit*. It is a syllable pause line:—

And give | us cates | ◡ fit | for coun|try swains.

CCCXXVI.

Persia, down her Volga by canoes.

Ib., IX, 269 (Greene and Peele, ed. Dyce, 170a).

In order to restore the metre Professor Wagner (l. c., 525) proposes to read *adown*. The metre, however, is quite correct; scan:—

Persia, | ◡ down | her Vol|ga by | canoes.

CCCXXVII.

Ah, Bungay, my Brazen Head is spoil'd.

Ib., XIII, 4 (Greene and Peele, ed. Dyce, 174b).

'Query, says Dyce *ad loc.*, 'Ah, Bungay, *ah*, my.' I think there is no need of such an addition; scan:—

Ah, Bun|gay, ⏊ | my bra|zen head | is spoil'd.

MARLOWE.

CCCXXVIII.

Faust. So Faustus hath
Already done; and holds this principle,
There is no chief but only Belzebub.

Doctor Faustus (Works, ed. Dyce, Lon. 1870,
in 1 vol., 83 b and 120 b).

Qy. arrange:—

Faust. So Faustus hath already done, and holds
This principle:
There is no chief but only Belzebub?

CCCXXIX.

For that security craves great Lucifer.

Ib., (Works, ed. Dyce, 86 a and 112 b).

This is the reading of the first quarto (1604). In the second
quarto (1616) the line is corrected by the omission of *great;*
no such correction, however, is needed, as *security* may well
be pronounced as a trisyllable (*secur'ty*).

CCCXXX.

And Faustus hath bequeath'd his soul to Lucifer.

Ib., (Works, ed. Dyce, 86 b and 113 a).

An apparent Alexandrine. *Lucifer* is to be read as a trisyllabic feminine ending.

CCCXXXI.

Faust. How! now in hell.
Nay, an this be hell, I'll willingly be damn'd here:
What! walking, disputing, &c.

But, leaving off this, let me have a wife,
The fairest maid in Germany;
For I am wanton and lascivious,
And cannot live without a wife.
  Meph. How! a wife!
I prithee, Faustus, talk not of a wife.
IB., (WORKS, ED. DYCE, 87a SEQ. AND 114a).

From a comparison of this reading of the first quarto with
that of the second, we may fairly conclude that the passage
in the poet's Ms stood as follows: —
  Faust. How now! In hell!
An this be hell, I'll willingly be damn'd.
What! Sleeping, eating, walking, and disputing!
But leaving off this, let me have a wife,
The fairest maid *there is* in Germany;
For I am wanton and lascivious,
And cannot live without a wife.
  Meph.   A wife?
I prithee, Faustus, talk not of a wife.

MARSTON.

CCCXXXII.

Gods bores, it wil not stick to fal off.
ANTONIO'S REVENGE, II, I (THE WORKS OF JOHN MARSTON,
ED. J. O. HALLIWELL, LON., 1856, I, 90).

Qy.: *God's* BONES, *it will not stick,* BUT *fall off*? In John
S. Keltie's, The Works of the British Dramatists (Edinburgh,
1875), 369 b, the oath '*God's bores*' has been omitted in
accordance with the editor's endeavour to purge from im-
purity the plays reprinted by him (Preface, VII).

CCCXXXIII.

Shee's most fair, true, most chaste, most false; because
Most faire, tis firme Ile marrie her.

Ib., II, 4, FIN. (WORKS, I, 102).

Read and arrange: —

She is most fair, *most* true, most chaste, most false;
Because most fair, 'tis firm I'll marry her.

———

CCCXXXIV.

His sight would make me gnash my teeth terribly.

THE INSATIATE COUNTESS, A. I, (WORKS, III, 115).

A transposition of the adverb *terribly* seems to be the only
means of reducing this line to something like metre: —

His sight | would *ter*|*r'bly* make | me gnash | my teeth.

———

CCCXXXV.

How like Adonis in his hunting weedes,
Lookes this same godesse-tempter?
And art thou come? This kisse enters into thy soule:
Gods, I doe not envy you; for know this
Way's here on earth compleat, excels your blisse:
Ile not change this nights pleasure with you all.

Ib., A. III, (WORKS, III, 155).

Read and arrange:—

How like Adonis in his hunting weeds,
Looks this same goddess-tempter? And art thou come?
This kiss enters into thy soul.
Gods, I *don't* envy you; for know *you* this:
What's here on earth complete, excels your bliss;
I'll not change this night's pleasure with you all. -

———

CCCXXXVI.

Women are made
Of blood, without soules; when their beauties fade,
And their lusts past, avarice or bawdry
Makes them still lov'd; then they buy venere,
Bribing damnation, and hire brothell slaves.

IB., A. III, AD FIN. (WORKS, III, 160).

Bawdry is either to be pronounced as a trisyllable
(*bawd-e-ry*), or we must transpose: *bawdry or avarice.* Instead of *venere* read *venery.* Qy. read *lust's?*

CCCXXXVII.

What Tanais, Nilus, or what Tioris swift,
What Rhenus ferier then the cataract,
Although Neptolis cold, the waves of all the Northerne Sea,
Should flow for ever through these guilty hands,
Yet the sanguinolent staine would extant be.

IB., A. V, (WORKS, III, 181).

Read and arrange:—

What Tanais, Nilus, or what *Tigris* swift,
What Rhenus *fiercer* than the cataract,
Can quench hell's fire? Although *Pactolus' gold,*
Although the waves of all the Northern Sea,
Should flow for ever through these guilty hands,
Yet the sanguinolent stain would extant be.

The context clearly shows that something like the words inserted has been lost after *cataract,* a suspicion which is confirmed by the irregularity of the metre, in so far as the line
Although Neptolis . . . . *Northerne Sea* must necessarily be broken
in two. The Tigris could not be characterized by a more

appropriate epithet than *swift*, as this river is renowned for
its rapid flow; its name means *arrow*. With respect to the
correction *Rhenus* FIERCER &c., Milton's *fierce Phlegeton* (Para-
dise Lost, II, 580) may be compared.— In writing this passage the poet evidently had before his mind's eye not only
a line from Horace (Epodes, XV, 20), but also the celebrated
soliloquy of Lady Macbeth (V, 1, 39 seqq.): Out, damned
spot! out, I say! . . . . . What, will these hands ne'er be
clean? &c. Shakespeare's 'Macbeth' is said to have been
first acted in 1610 (which I think too late a date), whilst
'The Insatiate Countess' was first published in 1613.

CCCXXXVIII.

Abi. Husband, I'le naile me to the earth, but I'le
Winne your pardon.
My jewels, jointure, all I have shall flye;
Apparell, bedding, I'le not leave a rugge,
So you may come off fairely.

IB., A. V, (WORKS, III, 191).

Read and arrange: —

Abi. Husband, I'll nail me to the earth, but *I*
Will win your pardon. My jewels, jointure, all
I have, shall fly; apparel, bedding, I'll
Not leave a rug, so you may come off fairly.

CCCXXXIX.

Tha[is]. Hee's stung already, as if his eyes were
turn'd on
Persies shield.

IB., A. V, (WORKS, III, 194).

Read, of course, PERSEUS' *shield.*

CCCXL.

Rog. Had I knowne this I would have poison'd thee
in the chalice
This morning, when we receaved the sacrament.
Cla. Slave, knowst thou this? tis an appendix to the
letter;
But the greater temptation is hidden within.
I will scowre thy gorge like a hawke : thou shalt swallow
thine owne stone in this letter, [*They bustle.*
Seal'd and delivered in the presence of —

IB., A. V, (WORKS, III, 195).

Read and arrange : —

Rog. Had I known this, I would have poison'd thee
This morning in the chalice, when we received
The sacrament.
Cla. Slave, know'st thou this? 'Tis an
Appendix to the letter; but the greater
Temptation 's *hid* within. *I'll* scour thy gorge
Like *to* a hawk [*hawk's* ?]:
Thou shalt swallow thine own stone in this letter,
Seal'd and deliver'd in the presence of—

[*They wrestle.*

SHAKESPEARE.

CCCXLI.

As if we had them not. Spirits are finely touch'd.

MEASURE FOR MEASURE, I, I, 36.

'In *Measure for Measure,* says Mr Fleay *apud* Ingleby,
Occasional Papers, &c., 84, the regular instances [viz. of
Alexandrines] are numerous and the change to the third

period complete.' Mr Fleay is quite right as to the frequency
in 'Measure for Measure' of that peculiar kind of verse which
he calls Alexandrines, and I differ from him only in so far
as I take the great majority of them to be blankverse,
mostly with a trisyllabic feminine ending either at the end
of the line, or at the end of the first hemistich, i. e. before
the pause. I am perfectly aware that Mr Fleay's opinions
on this head are shared more or less by most English
Shakespearians and prosodists, amongst others by Mr Alexander J. Ellis who in his elaborate work 'On Early English
Pronunciation' (III, 943 seq.) has proved a staunch defender
of Alexandrines in Shakespeare and an eager, though un-
successful antagonist of Dr Abbott. It would be labour thrown
away to argue with Mr Ellis and to examine the details of
his theory; I merely mention him lest, at some time or other,
my silence should be misinterpreted as ignorance. In the
following scansions I shall omit some few of the lines designated as Alexandrines by Mr Fleay and for brevity's sake
shall now and then mark the middle syllable of trisyllabic
feminine endings by an apostrophe. To begin with the line
at the head of this note, it has a trisyllabic feminine ending
before the pause (*had them not*), while *Spirits* is to be pronounced as a monosyllable.

I, 1, 56: Matters of needful value: we shall write to you.
    Hanmer omitted *to you*. Mr Fleay writes *t'you* and
    declares the line to be an Alexandrine 'with Spen-
    serian cesura.' In my opinion the verse should be
    scanned: —

    Matters | of need|ful val|ue: we sháll | write tó | you.
    Compare A. IV, sc. 3, l. 141 : —

    And gen|eral hon|our. I'm | direct|ed bý | you.

I, 3, 37: For what I bid them do: for we bid this be done.

Be done omitted by Pope. *Bid them do* is a trisyllabic feminine ending before the pause. Compare K. Richard III, I, 2, 89: —

> Say that | I slew | them not? Why, then | they
>   are | not dead,

and Coriolanus, IV, 1, 27: —

> As 'tis | to laugh | at 'em. My moth|er, you | wot well.

Possibly, however, all these lines may just as well be taken for what are termed trimeter couplets by Dr Abbott, s. 500 seq.

I, 3, 39: And not | the pun|'shment. Therefore, | indeed,
                                          my fath|er.

Indeed omitted by Pope.

I, 4, 5: Upon | the sist|'rhood, the vo|t'rists of | Saint Clare.

Pope *sister votaries;* Dyce *sisterhood, votarists.*

I, 4, 70: To sof|ten An|g'lo; and that's | my pith | of
                                          bus|'ness.

Pith of omitted by Pope; Hanmer and Dyce end the line at *pith* and thus complete the following line, although they differ in their readings.

II, 2, 9: Why dost thou ask again? Lest I might be too rash.

Dost thou omitted by Hanmer. *Ask again* seems to be a trisyllabic feminine ending; the line may, however, be taken for a trimeter couplet, just like II, 2, 12; II, 2, 14; II, 2, 41, and numerous others.

II, 2, 70: And what | a pris|'ner. Ay, touch | him; there's |
                                          the vein.

II, 2, 183: To sin in loving virtue: never could the strumpet.

Dyce and Mr Fleay justly adopt Pope's correction *ne'er* for *never* and thus make the line a regular blank-verse with an extra syllable before the pause.

II, 4, 118: T'have what | we would | have, we speak | not
                              what | we mean.
   Steevens (and Dyce) *we'd.*

II, 4, 128 (not 127): In prof|'ting by | them. Nay, call | us
                              ten | times frail.

II, 4, 153 seq. Pope, Dyce (and others?) justly end l. 153
   at *world.* Dyce thinks the word *aloud* an inter-
   polation and is surprised that none of the former editors has thrown it out. In my opinion such an omission
   would be quite uncalled for, as the two lines are thus
   to be scanned: —

   Or with | an out|stretch'd throat | I'll tell | the world
   Aloud | what man | thou 'rt.

            Ang.   Who will | believe | thee, Is|'bel?

   Both *man thou art* and *Isabel* are trisyllabic feminine
   endings; as to the latter compare IV, 3, 119; V, 1, 387;
   V, 1, 392, and V, 1, 435.

III, 1, 32 seq. Qy. arrange and scan: —

      For end|ing thee | no soon|er. Thou hast | nor youth
      Nor age, | but, as | 'twere, an af|ter-din|ner's sleep?

III, 1, 61: To-mor|row you|set on. | Is there | no rem|'dy?

III, 1, 89: In base|appli|'nces. This out|ward-saint|ed dep|'ty.
   Hanmer reads *appliance.*

III, 1, 151 (not 150): 'Tis best | that thou | diest quick|ly.
                              O hear | me, Is|'bel.
   The old copies as well as the modern editions, as far
   as they are known to me, wrongly read *Isabella.* The
   line has an extra syllable before the pause and a trisyllabic feminine ending.

IV, 2, 76 seqq.: The best and wholesomest spirits of the night
Envelop you, good Provost. Who call'd here of late?
Prov. None, since the curfew rung.
, *Duke.* Not Isabel? ˙
Prov.   No.   ˙.   ˙
, *Duke.*   ,·They will, then, ere't be long.
Arrange: —.:.
ˮ The best and wholesomest spirits of the night
Envelop you, good Provost! Who call'd here
Of late? :˙
⁰¹   *Prov.* None, since the curfew rung.   ˙
,   *Duke.*   , Not Isabel?
ˉ *Prov.* No.   ˙
Duke. *She* will, then, ere't be long.
Isabel is a trisyllabic feminine ending or a quasi-dis-
syllable; compare The Works of John Marston, ed.
J. O. Halliwell (London, 1856) III, 110:—
Isabell | advan|ces to | a sec|ond bed.
Of late.... Isabel, therefore, is a regular blankverse
and the Alexandrine is discarded. *They,* in the last
line, has rightly been altered to *She* by Hawkins.
Compare Abbott, s. 501.   ˙
IV, 2, 86 seq.: To qualify in others: were he mealed with that
·˙ Which he corrects, then were he tyrannous.
In the one-volume edition of Shakespeare's Plays and
⁰¹˙ ˙˙ Poems published by Ernest Fleischer, Leipsic, 1833,
the words *with that* are transferred to the following
line and I am surprised that this correction has not
been recorded in the Cambridge Edition. Mr Fleay
recommends the same transposition and it only remains
to add, that *tyrannous* is a trisyllabic feminine ending
which makes the line a correct blankverse.

IV, 2, 103: Profess'd | the con|tr'ry. This is | his lord|ship's man.
IV, 3, 131: By every syllable a faithful verity.
>Strange to say, this line is not mentioned by Mr Fleay.
>*Verily* is a trisyllabic feminine ending; compare *supra*
>No. CLXXXI.

IV, 3, 137: There to give up their power. If you can, pace
>>>>>>>>>>>>>>>>>your wisdom.
>I strongly suspect that the words *If you can* did not
>come from the poet's pen and should be struck out.

IV, 3, 145: At Mariana's house to-night. Her cause and yours.
>*To-night* omitted by Pope. Mr Fleay rightly, though
>diffidently, suggests *Marian's*, and thus restores a regu-
>lar blankverse. It has not occurred to Mr Fleay that
>the same correction is to be applied to A. V, sc. 1,
>l. 379 and A. V, sc. 1, l. 408:—
>>Is all | the grace | I beg. | Come hith|er, Ma|rian.
>>For Ma|rian's sake: | but as | he adjudg'd | your
>>>>>>>>>>>>>>>>>>>>broth|er.

IV, 5, 6: As cause | doth min|'ster. Go, call | at Fla|vius' house.
>*Go* omitted by Hanmer.

V, 1, 32: Or wring redress from you. Hear me, O hear me, here!
>Dyce justly queries *here*; it is certainly an interpolation.

V, 1, 42: Is it not strange and strange? Nay, it is ten
>>>>>>>>>>>>>>>>>times strange.
>Omit, with Pope, Dyce, &c. *it is.*

V, 1, 51: That I | am touch'd | with mad|ness. Make not |
>>>>>>>>>>>>>>>>impossl|'ble.

V, 1, 54 (not 56): May seem | as shy, | as grave, | as just, |
>>>>>>>>>>>>>>>>as ab|s'lute.

V, 1, 65: For in|equal|'ty; but let | your rea|son serve.
>Pope needlessly transferred *serve* to the beginning of
>the next line in which he omitted the article before *truth.*

V, 1, 74: As then | the mess|'nger, — That's I, | an 't like|
your grace.

As to *messenger* see S. Walker, Versif., 200 seq.

V, 1, 101: And I | did yield | t' him: but the | next morn | betimes. *But the* omitted by Pope. *Yield to him* is a trisyllabic feminine ending before the pause.

V, 1, 233: A mar|ble mon|'ment. I did | but smile | till now.

V, 1, 260: Upon | these slan|d'rers: My lord, | we'll do | it
through|ly.

————

CCCXLII.

Cap. It is perchance that you yourself were saved.

TWELFTH NIGHT, I, 2, 6.

This line should be spoken by one of the Sailors, to whom Viola has expressly addressed herself; *what think you, sailors?* she asks. I have no doubt that the speech was transferred to the Captain by the actors merely for want of a player capable of impersonating a '*First Sailor,*' the representatives of the Sailors being what were called hired men and unfit to take part in the dialogue, such as now-a-days are termed walking gentlemen. Similar combinations of different characters for want of a sufficient number of actors are by no means of rare occurrence; two very striking instances occur, the one in A. II, sc. 4 of the present play (see *infra* note CCCLVI), the other in K. Lear, IV, 7, where the Doctor and the Gentleman 'are distinct characters, and have separate prefixes' in the Quartos, whilst 'according to the folio, the two parts were combined, and played by the same actor' (see Collier's note *ad loc.*).

————

CCCXLIII.

> ▲   After our ship did split,
> When you and those poor number saved with you
> Hung on our driving boat, I saw your brother.
>
> IB., I, 2, 9 SEQQ.

Instead of *those* Rowe (2ᵈ ed.) reads *that*; Capell *this*; *the*
Anon. conj. Qy. read: —

> After our ship did split,
> When you and those — poor number! — saved with you
> Hung on our driving boat, &c.?

———

CCCXLIV.

> The like of him. Know'st thou this country?
>
> IB., I, 2, 21.

With the help of a slight alteration this verse may be
scanned as a syllable pause line: —

The like | of him. | ∪ Know|est thou | this coun|try.

There is, however, only one more line contained in the present play which might possibly allow of being classed with
this category of verses, viz. V, I, 226: —

How have | the hours | ∪ rack'd | and tor|tured me.

This circumstance must put us on our guard so much the
more as both lines admit of a different and almost easier
scansion by the well-known introduction of an additional syllable in *country* and *hours*: —

The like | of him. | Know'st thou | this coun|t(e)ry

and: —

How have | the hou|(e)rs rack'd | and tor|tur'd me.

These scansions are supported by A. I, sc. I, l. 32: —

And last|ing in | her sad | remem|b(e)rance.

Under these circumstances, I think, I shall be justified in asserting that Twelfth Night is free from syllable pause lines, whereas they abound e. g. in Antony and Cleopatra, in Cymbeline, and Pericles. To me this seems to be a most momentous fact, apt to be made a starting-point for further metrical disquisitions and to be admitted among what are called metrical tests.

CCCXLV.

Sir And. What is 'pourquoi'? do or not do? I would I had bestowed that time in the tongues that I have in fencing, dancing and bear-baiting: O, had I but followed the arts!

Sir To. Then hadst thou had an excellent head of hair.

Sir And. Why, would that have mended my hair?

Sir To. Past question; for thou seest it will not curl by nature.

Sir And. But it becomes me well enough, does't not?

Sir To. Excellent; it hangs like flax on a distaff; &c.

IB., I, 3, 96 SEQQ.

'The point of Sir Toby's jest, remarks Dr Aldis Wright *ad loc.*, will be lost unless we remember that "tongues" and "tongs" were pronounced alike, as was pointed out by Mr Crosby of Zainsville [Zanesville] in the American Bibliopolist, June, 1875 [p. 143].' — This ingenious explanation, though it can hardly be disputed, does not preclude the existence of a second quibble between *arts* and *hards*, i. e. tow.

CCCXLVI.

Sir To. Wherefore are these things hid? wherefore have these gifts a curtain before 'em? are they like to take dust, like Mistress Mall's picture?

IB., I, 3, 133 SEQQ.

2 *

It seems chronologically impossible to me that this passage
should refer to Moll Cutpurse (Mary Frith). Moll Cutpurse
is generally said to have been born in 1584 (or even so late
as 1589); consequently she was between 17. and 18. years
old when Twelfth Night was performed at the Middle Temple
on Feb. 2, 1601—2. At that time she did not yet enjoy the
notoriety which made her the heroine of John Day's 'Maddo
pranckes of mery Mall of the Banckside' in 1610, and of
Middleton and Dekker's 'Roaring Girl' in 1611. These were
no doubt the years when she had reached the height of her
disreputable career and become of sufficient interest to have
her portrait prefixed as a frontispiece to Middleton and
Dekker's play. I cannot think that she should ever have
been thought a worthy subject for the painter's brush; nor
can I subscribe to the explanations given by Dyce, but fully
agree with Mr John Fitchett Marsh who shows that 'Mistress
Mall' is Maria, Olivia's gentlewoman (N. and Q., July 6 and
Nov. 30, 1878). Maria is certainly not a common servant,
but in part at least a confidante of her mistress, and her
picture, executed not in oil, but in watercolours and done
perhaps when she was in her teens, may well be imagined
hanging in the room where Sir Toby and his weak-brained
friend sit carousing, a room which does by no means belong
to Olivia's drawing-rooms, but is something between a parlour
and a buttery; perhaps it is even Maria's own parlour.
Maria does not seem to care much for her picture; it is
neglected and covered with dust. For be it remarked, Sir
Toby does not at all say that Mistress Mall's picture is cur-
tained, but that it has taken dust, a circumstance which, for
all I know, has been overlooked or misinterpreted by all
editors.

CCCXLVII.

Vio. On your attendance, my lord; here.

IB., I, 4, 11.

A slight transposition would certainly improve the line: —

On your attendance; *here, my lord.*

CCCXLVIII.

Oli. Cousin, cousin, how have you come so early by this lethargy?

IB., I, 5, 131 SEQ.

Either intentionally or unintentionally Olivia mistakes Sir Toby's belching for yawning.

CCCXLIX.

I pray you, tell me if this be the lady of the house, for I never saw her.

IB.; I, 5, 182 SEQ.

Before the words, *I pray you* &c. a stage-direction, be it either, *To Maria*, or, *To the Attendants* should be added.

CCCL.

Oli. Have you any commission from your lord to negotiate with my face? You are now out of your text: but we will draw the curtain and show you the picture. Look you, sir, such a one I was this present: is 't not well done? [*Unveiling.*

IB., I, 5, 249 SEQQ.

Of all attempts at healing the corruption of the last sentence, one only has succeeded, viz. that made by Theobald:

such a one I WEAR *this present,* which, in my judgment, is
undoubtedly the true reading. For the rest compare Westward Ho!, II, 3, init.: *Sir Gos[ling].* So, draw those curtains,
and let's see the pictures under them. [*The ladies unmask.*

———

CCCLI.

Thy tongue, thy face, thy limbs, actions and spirit,
Do give thee five-fold blazon: not too fast: soft, soft!
Unless the master were the man. How now!
Even so quickly may one catch the plague?

IB., I, 5, 311 SEQQ.

The twofold exclamation, *Soft, soft!* has been placed in an
interjectional line by Dyce and regular metre has thus been
restored. In my opinion, however, the chief break in Olivia's
speech occurs in the next line and I should, therefore, prefer
the following arrangement: —

Thy tongue, thy face, thy limbs, actions and spirit,
Do give thee five-fold blazon: not too fast!
Soft, soft!— unless the master were the man!
How now!
Even so quickly may one catch the plague?

Either of these two arrangements, Dyce's and mine, removes
the Alexandrine and consequently one of them should be
installed in the text.

———

CCCLII.

Mal. She returns this ring to you, sir: you might have
saved me my pains, to have taken it away yourself. She

adds, moreover, that you should put your lord into a desperate assurance she will none of him.

IB., II, 2, 5 SEQQ.

After *sir* Hanmer inserted the following clause: *for being your Lord's she'll none of it,* and some such insertion seems indeed to be required, as in I, 5, 321 Olivia charges Malvolio to tell Cesario, that she will none of it, viz. the ring, and in II, 2, 25 Cesario, in his soliloquy, repeats the words, *None of my lord's ring,* as having come from Olivia through her 'churlish messenger'. I, therefore, think it most likely that the missing words were, *she will none of your lord's ring.* This insertion, however, does not suffice to restore the passage, but at the same time renders a correction of the words, *she will none of him,* unavoidable, especially as they do not come from Olivia. Olivia says (I, 5, 323): *I am not for him,* and we expect to hear Malvolio repeat these very words. The passage as I imagine it to have been written by the poet, will then read thus: 'She returns this ring to you, sir; *she will none of your lord's ring.* You might have saved me my pains, to have taken it away yourself. She adds, moreover, that you should put your lord into a desperate assurance *she is not for him.*'

———

CCCLIII.

Sir To. We did keep time, sir, in our catches. Sneck up!

IB., II, 2, 101.

Theobald is quite right in adding the stage-direction: *Hiccoughs.* In order to produce the greatest possible similarity of sound we should write: *Snick up (Snick up — hiccup).*

———

CCCLIV.

Sir. To. Out o' tune sir, ye lye:

IB., II, 3, 122.

This reading of the Ff should never have been disturbed, except with respect to the pointing, in so far as an interrogation should be substituted for the comma after *sir*, and an exclamation for the colon after *lye*; moreover a comma is to be added after *tune*. The words are addressed to the clown who has roused Sir Toby's bile by telling him that he dares not 'bid him [Malvolio] go.' This impertinent remark, Sir Toby says, is 'out of tune' and a lie, and to prove it so he forthwith bounces upon Malvolio exhorting him not to overstep the bounds of his office as steward; after which he roundly bids him go: 'Go, sir, rub your chain with crums.' In order to exclude every doubt, two stage-directions might be added, viz.: *To the Clown* (before, *Out o' tune*) and *To Malvolio* (before, *Art any more* &c.).

CCCLV.

Sir To. She's a beagle, true-bred, and one that adores me: what o' that?

IB., II, 3, 195.

Dr Aldis Wright has ingeniously pointed out that Maria is of diminutive stature and is chaffed on that account first by Viola (I, 5, 218: *Some mitigation for your giant, sweet lady*) and afterwards by Sir Toby (II, 3, 193: *Good night, Penthesilea*). He might have added the present line, for according to all old and modern authorities a beagle was — or is — a small dog. See Skeat, Etym. Dict., s. Beagle. It was used as a term of endearment and applied to persons of either sex; compare Dekker and Webster's Westward Ho, III, 4, init., where Mrs Tenterhook says to Mr Monopoly: *You are. a sweet beagle.* The brevity of Maria's person is also alluded~to~in A. II, sc. 5, l. 16: *Here comes~the little villain,* and in A. III, sc. 1, l. 70 seq.: *Look, where, the youngest wren of nine comes.*

CCCLVI.

Now, good Cesario, but that piece of song,
That old and antique song we heard last night: &c.

Ib., II, 4, 2 SEQ.

This request of the Duke is replied to, not by Cesario, but by Curio, a subordinate character, who informs his master that he, who should sing it, viz. Olivia's fool, is not here. But the Duke did not want to hear the Clown sing, but Cesario, who in A. I, sc. 2, l. 67 seq. has assured the Captain that he

'can sing

And speak to him [the Duke] in many sorts of music.'
And what business and right has Lady Olivia's fool to sing before the Duke? After being introduced by Curio (l. 41) he is desired by Orsino almost in the same words as Cesario was some minutes ago, to sing 'the song we had last night.' Now, who was last night's singer? Cesario or the Clown? And why does not Cesario sing when desired by his master to do so? — It seems evident that according to the poet's intention two singers were required for the performance of our play: the one to sing in Orsino's palace (the performer of Viola) and the other to do the same office in Lady Olivia's house (the Clown). As, however, at some time or other, the Lord Chamberlain's men could only boast of a single singer and that one the Clown, they gave him access to the Duke's

palace and made him do the singing of both parts. Compare *supra* note CCCXLII.

CCCLVII.

Sir To. Come thy ways, Signior Fabian.

IB., II, 5, 1.

In A. II, sc. 3, l. 188 Maria proposes to plant the two knights, 'and let the fool make a third', where Malvolio shall find the letter. In the present scene they are being planted in Olivia's garden, but it is not the fool who makes the third, but Fabian. who is only now introduced to the reader. As Fabian has been brought out of favour with my lady by Malvolio, he is indeed a more legitimate partner in the conspiracy, or, to say the least, a more deeply interested witness than the Clown of the severe joke practised on the puritanical and malevolent steward whose name is by no means meaningless. But if this was the poet's design from the beginning, why did he make Maria mention the Clown as a third partaker? She might just as well have hit on Fabian as companion of the two knights, so much the more as she must have been aware how eager a spectator he would be and that he would consider her joke a fit retribution. I confess myself unable to clear away this difficulty.

CCCLVIII.

Sir To. Here comes the little villain. [*Enter Maria.*] How now, my metal of India?

IB., II, 5, 16 SEQ.

'My metal of India' cannot possibly be the true reading, for the following reasons. 1. It cannot be shown that 'metal', without some epithet intimating such a meaning, was ever

used in the sense of 'gold'. Such a meaning, in my humble
opinion, is a purely gratuitous assumption for the nonce.
2. India is not, and never was, rich in gold, as California
and Australia are now-a-days. It abounds, however, in precious stones of the greatest beauty and value, and Shakespeare,
had he wished to compare Maria to some Indian treasure,
would certainly have bethought himself of those renowned
Indian jewels and diamonds instead of an Indian metal.
3. The metaphor does not apply to Maria in a higher degree
than to almost all persons of the female sex. 4. It is not
at all in Sir Toby's vein to compliment Maria in good earnest;
on the contrary he keeps continually teasing her and has just
now styled her 'a little villain'. Under the circumstances I
am fully persuaded that the later Ff exhibit the correct reading,
viz. 'my *nettle* of India,' and completely agree with what has
been advanced on this head by Singer in his note ad *loc.*
The nettle of India may possibly be the *Urtica crenulata*
which is a native of Bengal; see Heinr. Gräfe, *Handbuch der
Naturgeschichte der drei Reiche* &c. (Eisleben und Leipzig,
1838) Vol. II a, p. 630. However that may be, at all
events Maria may well be termed a little 'stinging nettle'
(K. Richard II, III, 2, 18); by her plot she stings Malvolio to
the quick and she proves not much less prickly to the Clown,
to Sir Andrew and to Cesario whom in A. I, sc. 5, l. 215
she desires to 'hoist sail'. Who knows but even Sir Toby,
with whom she is in love, may have experienced not only
her quick wit, but also her sharp tongue; that she is sharp-
tongued is admitted by Dr Aldis Wright in his note on A. II,
sc. 5, l. 139. The Rev. Henry N. Ellacombe (The Plant-
Lore and Garden-Craft of Shakespeare, Exeter, 1878, p. 137)
seems not to have been acquainted with Singer's note.

CCCLIX.

Mal. There is example for 't; the lady of the Strachy married the yeoman of the wardrobe.

IB.; II, 5, 44 SEQ.

'The incident of a lady of high rank, Dr Aldis Wright says in his note *ad loc.*, marrying a servant is the subject of Webster's Duchess of Malfi, who married the steward of her household, and would thus have supplied Malvolio with the exact parallel to his own case of which he was in search.' It seems most strange to me that Dr Aldis Wright should not have concluded this remark with substituting the '*lady of* MALFY' in the room of the 'lady of the Strachy' who owes her existence no doubt to a mistake of one of those privileged blunderers, viz. the transcribers and compositors. Why may not Shakespeare have read the story of the Duchess of Malfy in Paynter's Palace of Pleasure just as well as Webster? Certainly nothing could fall in more naturally with the context than the lady of *Malfy*, whereas the conjectural emendations on this passage chronicled in the Cambridge and Clarendon editions are singularly far-fetched and almost all of them worse than the lection of the Ff itself.

CCCLX.

Fab. Now is the woodcock near the gin.

Sir To. O, peace! and the spirit of humours intimate reading aloud to him!

IB., II, 5, 92 SEQQ.

A nice discrimination between the characters of Fabian and Sir Toby leads to the suspicion that the prefixes of these two speeches have most likely been transposed and should be altered. Just as, according to the Cambridge

Editors, ll. 39 and 43, in which peace is enjoined on Sir Andrew, belong to Fabian, so l. 92, which urges silence on Sir Toby, should be assigned to the same character, whose eagerness to hear the contents of the letter is naturally greater than Sir Toby's, this latter being in the secret. Read therefore: —

Sir To. Now is the woodcock near the gin.

Fab. O, peace! and the spirit of humours intimate reading aloud to him!

CCCLXI.

Vio. Save thee, friend, and thy music: dost thou live by thy tabor?

Iʙ., III, ɪ, ɪ ꜱᴇꞯ.

Thus FA; the true reading, however, is that of the later Ff: *dost thou live by* THE *tabor*, as there is certainly a play upon *tabor* which besides signifying a drum, was also used as the sign or name of an inn. According to Collier *ad loc.* 'the Clown's reply, "No, sir; I live by the Church," is not intelligible, if we do not suppose him to have wilfully misunderstood Viola to ask whether he lived near the sign of the tabor.' Very true, but if so, Collier should not have retained the reading of the first Folio, by which such a quibble is precluded.

CCCLXII.

Grace and good disposition attend your ladyship.

Iʙ., III, ɪ, 146.

Hanmer most boldly reads *you* instead of *your ladyship* and the editors of the Globe Edition have adopted a different division of the lines, proposed by S. Walker, Crit. Exam. III, 87. However this deviation from the old copies seems to be unwarranted, as *ladyship* may well be taken to be a trisyllabic feminine ending; scan: —

Grace and | good dis|posi|tion attend | your la|dyship.

Compare A. III, sc. 3, l. 24 (*pardon me*); A. III, sc. 3, l. 35 (*city did*); A. III, sc. 4, l. 383 (*misery*); A. IV, sc. 3, l. 17 (*followers*); A. IV, sc. 3, l. 21 (*deceivable*); A. V, sc. 1, l. 75 (*enemies*); and A. V, sc. 1, l. 79 (*enemy*). — It need hardly be added that the line has an extra syllable before the pause. Some editors print *'tend* or *tend*, which, after all, may be right.

CCCLXIII.

Oli. O, what a deal of scorn looks beautiful &c.

IB., III, 1, 157.

Staunton and the Rev. H. Hudson justly add the stage-direction: *Aside*, which cannot be missed.

CCCLXIV.

Oli. Yet come again; for thou perhaps mayst move
That heart, which now abhors, to like his love.

IB., III, 1, 175 SEQ.

The editors, as far as I know them, keep *altum silentium* about this passage, which to them seems to offer no difficulty whatever. Schlegel and Gildemeister, both of them classical translators, refer 'that heart' to Olivia's heart, which perhaps may be moved to like his love, i. e. Orsino. But may not Olivia be presumed with far greater probability to express a hope that Cesario, if coming back, may move his own heart to like his love, i. e. Olivia, whom it now abhors? Schlegel renders the lines as follows: —

O komm zurück! Du magst dies Herz bethören,
Ihn, dessen Lieb' es hasst, noch zu erhören.
In my judgment it should be: —

O komm zurück! Du magst DEIN *Herz bethören,*
SIE, DEREN *Lieb' es hasst, noch zu erhören.*
Gildemeister's version might no less easily be altered. According to him Olivia says: —

Komm wieder nur, du rührst mein Herz vielleicht,
Dass es für den Verhassten sich erweicht.
Should it not rather be: —

Komm wieder nur, du rührst DEIN *Herz vielleicht,*
Dass es für DIE VERHASSTE *sich erweicht?*

CCCLXV.

Oli. I have sent after him: he says he'll come;
How shall I feast him? what bestow of him?
For youth is bought more oft than begg'd or borrow'd.
I speak too loud.
                                                IB., III, 4, I SEQQ.

The words: *he says he'll come* are 'explained by Warburton to mean "I suppose now, or admit now, he says he'll come, &c.". Dyce *ad loc.* According to Mr Rolfe *ad loc.* they are 'apparently = Suppose he says he'll come.' In my opinion this is too strained an explanation as to be acceptable or even grammatically admissible. 'Theobald, Mr Rolfe continues, made it read "*Say, he* will come."' The Rev. H. Hudson grants that 'the concessive sense is evidently required, not the affirmative' and 'that the simple transposition [*says he* instead of *he says*] gets the same sense [as Theobald's alteration] naturally enough; the subjunctive being

often formed in that way.' I think differently. The first four
lines are evidently spoken aside by Olivia, as confirmed by
her own words, *I speak too loud*; only in the fifth line she
addresses Maria. It is, however, in the natural course of
things that she should have conversed with Maria on the
subject before and that the latter should have tried to raise
the drooping spirit of her enamoured mistress by consol-
atory words. I should accordingly feel no hesitation in
reading:—

    Oli. [*Aside*]. I have sent after him: *she* says he'll come;
How shall I feast him? what bestow of him?
For youth is bought more oft than begg'd or borrow'd.
I speak too loud.
[*To Maria*] Where is Malvolio? &c.

Olivia may easily be imagined to accompany the words, *she
says he'll come* with a slight motion of either hand or head
towards Maria.

—————

CCCLXVI.

    Sec. Off. Come, sir, I pray you, go.
    Ant. Let me speak a little. This youth that you see here
I snatch'd one half out of the jaws of death &c.

                       IB., III, 4, 392 SEQQ.

All critical efforts notwithstanding l. 393 has remained a
metrical stumbling block. The words *a little*, besides spoiling
the metre, impress the reader as ridiculously superfluous and
have probably slipped from their original place which was in
the second half of the preceding line, for I have little doubt
that in the poet's manuscript this line was complete, exactly
as it is the case with lines 381, 386, and 391 of this very

scene. In a word, I suspect the original wording of the passage to have been somewhat to the following effect: —

Sec. Off. Come, sir, I pray you, go.

Ant.   *Tarry a little*

And let me speak. This youth that you see here &c.

Stay but a little would, of course, do equally well as *Tarry a little.*

CCCLXVII.

Sir To. Hold, sir, or I'll throw your dagger o'er the house.

.IB., IV, 1, 30 SEQ.

From these words it appears that Sebastian is belabouring
Sir Andrew with his dagger; daggers, in the time of Elizabeth, were long enough to be used for such a purpose.

CCCLXVIII.

Like a mad lad,

Pare thy nails, dad;

Adieu, goodman devil.

IB., IV, 2, 139 SEQQ.

The only critic that ever took exception at this reading of
the old copies, is Dr Farmer who proposed to put an interrogation after *dad.* In my humble opinion the text is corrupt; the poet possibly wrote *Pares,* although I suggest it not
without diffidence. *Pares* would refer to the old Vice, Who
.... Cries, ah, ha! to the devil: and Like a mad lad Pares
thy nails, dad; *dad* being meant for the devil. It was a
favourite trick of the Vice to pare the devil's nails with his
dagger; see K. Henry V, IV, 4, 76: Bardolph and Nym had
ten times more valour than this roaring devil i' the old play,
that every one may pare his nails with a wooden dagger.

3

Should the words *Pare thy nails*, *dad* be thought an exhortation addressed to Malvolio, it would be difficult to show in how far he could be likened to a mad lad on that account, as it is rather the act of a good, than a mad, lad to pare his nails.

————

CCCLXIX.

Oli. If it be aught to the old tune, my lord,
It is as fat and fulsome to mine ear
As howling after music.
   Duke.   Still so cruel?
   Oli. Still so constant, lord?
   Duke. What, to perverseness? &c.

                    IB., V, I, III SEQQ.

Mr P. A. Daniel (Notes and Conjectural Emendations of Certain Doubtful Passages in Shakespeare's Plays, 1870, p. 43) ingeniously proposes to add '*lady*' to the Duke's question: *Still so cruel?* Mr Daniel is right in so far as he has felt the want of an even balance in the two short speeches of the Duke and Lady Olivia, but his addition is an incumbrance on the metre and the equipoise of the two speeches may be attained just as well by the omission of '*lord*' (after *constant*) as by the addition of '*lady*'. One of these two conjectural emendations, either Mr Daniel's or mine, should be adopted; if Mr Daniel's, the Duke's speech should not be joined to the preceding verse, but form a short line by itself.

————

CCCLXX.

Vio. If nothing lets to make us happy both
But this my masculine usurp'd attire,

Do not embrace me till each circumstance
Of place, time, fortune, do cohere and jump
That I am Viola: which to confirm,
I'll bring you to a captain in this town,
Where lie my maiden weeds; by whose gentle help
I was preserved to serve this noble count.

IB., V, I, 256.

Viola is here made to speak nonsense. 'If nothing lets to make us happy', she says to Sebastian who, being now convinced of his sister's identity, is eager to embrace her as such, 'but my masculine attire, then do *not* embrace me' &c., instead of saying the very contrary, viz. then you may safely embrace me, for I have only usurped this boys' dress and my maiden weeds are lying at a captain's house in this town. Arrange, therefore: —

    Vio. Do not embrace me till each circumstance
Of place, time, fortune, do cohere and jump
That I am Viola: which to confirm, —
If nothing lets to make us happy .both
But this my masculine usurp'd attire, —
I'll bring you to a captain in this town,
Where lie my maiden weeds; by whose gentle help
I was preserved to serve this noble count.

I should add by the way, that the two conjectural emendations *maid's* and *preferr'd* instead of *maiden* and *preserved* seem to admit of little doubt.

———

CCCLXXI.

May be prevented now. The princes, France and Burgundy.

K. LEAR, I, I, 46.

There are few instances in Mr Fleay's list of Alexandrines in King Lear that cannot be shown without difficulty to be

3 *

either regular blankverse or what Dr Abbott terms trimeter couplets. The safest and most correct way will be to follow Mr Fleay step by step (with some few omissions), in order to enable the reader to judge for himself. As to the line quoted above, it contains two trisyllabic feminine endings, the one at the end of the first hemistich (*prevented now*; see Abbott, s. 472), the other at the end of the line (*Burgundy*; see S. Walker, Versification, 240 seqq.). Hanmer needlessly suggested to omit *now*.

I, 1, 94: My heart | into | my mouth: | I love | your maj||'sty.
See S. Walker, Versification, 174 seq.

I, 1, 109: So young, and so untender? So young, my lord, and true.
These are two short lines that should not be joined into one; the arrangement of the Cambridge and Globe Editions is right.

I, 1, 134: That troop | with maj||'sty. Ourself, | by month|ly course.

I, 1, 139: The swáy, | revén|ue, ex'cú|tion óf | the rést.
Compare my edition of Shakespeare's Tragedy of Hamlet (1882), p. 182, where a different, but less correct, scansion of this line has been given.

I, 1, 156 (not 155): Reverbs | no hol||l'wness. Kent, on| thy life, | no more.
See *supra* note CCCIV.

I, 1, 158: To wage | against | thine en||'mies; nor fear | to lose | it.

I, 1, 196: Or cease | your quest | of love? | Most roy|al maj||'sty.

I, 1, 198: Nor will | you ten|der less. | Right no|ble Bur|g'ndy.

I, 1, 226: Could nev|er plant | in me. I yet | beseech| your maj||'sty.

Trisyllabic feminine endings both before the pause
(*plant in me*) and at the end of the line (*majesty*).
Possibly, however, another scansion might be set up
against the triple ending of the first hemistich, viz.: --
> Could ne'er | plant in | me. I yet | beseech | your
> maj|'sty.

I, 1, 228: To speak | and pur|pose not; since what | I
well | intend.
Trisyllabic feminine ending before the pause; compare
Abbott, s. 471.

I, 1, 248: Duchess of Burgundy.— Nothing: I have sworn;
I am firm.
Either two short lines, as printed in the Cambridge
and Globe Editions, or *Burgundy* to be read as a
trisyllabic feminine ending before the pause and *I have*
and *I am* to be contracted: —
> Duchess | of Bur|g'ndy. Nothing: | I've sworn; | I'm firm.

I, 1, 250: That you | must lose | a hus|band. Peace be|
with Bur|g'ndy.

I, 1, 270: Come, no|ble Bur|g'ndy. — Bid fare|well to|
your sis|ters.

I, 2, 4: The cu|rios'ty | of na|tions to | deprive | me.
Pope reads *nicely*; Thirlby suggested *curtesie*, which
was adopted by Theobald. Mr Fleay's scansion is
right; compare S. Walker, Versification, 201, and *supra*
note CXIII.

I, 3, 23: What grows | o't, no mat|ter; advise | your fel|lows so.
Grows of it is a trisyllabic feminine ending before
the pause. The line admits, however, of another
scansion, viz.: —
> What grows | of it, | no mat|ter; advise | your fel|lows so.

Fellows so to be read as a trisyllabic feminine ending.

I, 4, 223: In rank and not-to-be endurèd riots. Sir.
Sir was rightly thrown out by Theobald. S. Walker,
Versification, 270, would place it in an interjectional line.

I, 4, 265: Shows like | a ri't|'s inn: epi|curism | and lust.
Steevens omitted *riotous*. *Riotous inn* is a trisyllabic
feminine ending before the pause.

I, 4, 347: At point | a hund|red knights: yes, that, | on
ev|'ry dream.
At point, omitted by Pope. *Hundred knights* seems to
be a trisyllabic feminine ending.

II, 1, 118 seq. Rightly arranged by Jennens: —
You we first seize on. I shall serve you truly,
However else. — For him I thank your grace.

II, 2, 79: Who wears | no hon|'sty. Such smi|ling rogues|
as these.
Pope transferred *as these* to the beginning of the following line, whilst Hanmer omitted these words.

II, 2, 91: Two short lines, as printed in the Globe Edition.

II, 2, 121: The same.

II, 2, 144: You should | not use | me so. Sir, being | his
knave, | I will.
Use me so is a trisyllabic feminine ending before the pause

II, 2, 177: Losses | their rem|'dies. All wea|ry and | o'er-
watch'd.

II, 4, 157: Age is | unne'|ss'ry: on | my knees | I beg.
This is S. Walker's scansion (Versif., 275), rightly
adopted by Mr Fleay.

II, 4, 234: I and | my hund|red knights. | Not al|toge'er | so.
See S. Walker, Versif., 103 seq. and note on IV, 7, 54.

III, 2, 67: Their scant|ed court|'sy. My wits | begin | to turn.

III, 4, 176: I do beseech your grace. — O, cry you mercy, sir.
The Qq rightly omit *sir*.

III, 4, 179: In, fellow, there, into the hovel: keep thee warm.
QA and Ff: *there, into th'*; QB: *there, in't*; Capell:
there, to the. — Read, point, and scan: —
In, fel|low: there | i' th' ho|vel keep | thee warm.

IV, 6, 145: And my | heart breaks | at it. Read. What, | wi'
th' case | of eyes.
Breaks at it is a trisyllabic feminine ending before
the pause.

IV, 6, 198: Scan either: —
I'm cut | to th' brains. | You shall | have an|ything.
or: —
I am | cut to | the brains. | You shall | have an|'thing.

IV, 6, 256: Upon | the Brit|ish par|ty. O, untime|ly death.
Hanmer: *On th' English, English* being the reading
of the Ff. The first two syllables of *O, untimely*
'coalesce or are rapidly pronounced together.' Abbott, s. 462.

IV, 7, 54: To see | ano'er | thus. I know | not what | to say.
To say, omitted by Hanmer. See Abbott, s. 466 and
supra note on II, 4, 234.

V, 3, 45: May equally determine. Sir, I thought it fit.
Read, with Pope, *thought fit.*

V, 3, 178: Did hate thee or thy father! Worthy prince,
I know 't.
I know 't is to be transferred to the beginning of the
following line, as printed by Hanmer, who moreover
completes l. 179 by reading, *I know it well.*

V, 3, 271: Corde|lia! Corde|lia, stay | a lit|tle. Ha!
The line has an extra syllable before the first pause.

V, 3, 295: Edmund | is dead, | m'lord. That's but | a
tri|fle here.

Pope, Theobald, Hanmer, and Warburton omit *here*.
Compare Pericles, I, 2, 101: —
> Well, m' lord, | since you | have given | me leave |
> to speak.

V, 3, 313: Vex not his ghost. Oh, let him pass! he hates
him much.

Much, which is only contained in QB, has been justly
omitted by almost all editors and should not have
been conjured up again by Mr Fleay.

———

CCCLXXII.

Call in the messengers. As I am Egypt's queen.

ANTONY AND CLEOPATRA, I, 1, 29.

Messengers, in this line, and *homager*, in the next but one,
are trisyllabic feminine endings before the pause; compare
note on Measure for Measure, V, 1, 74. Mr Fleay has added
l. 31 to his list of Alexandrines in Shakespeare, but no mention of l. 29 is made by him. — I take this opportunity of
mentioning that the term 'trisyllabic feminine ending' which
is objected to as an 'awkward phrase' by a writer in the
Saturday Review (November 22, 1884, p. 667 seq.) has been
introduced, for all I know, by Mr Fleay, (e. g. *apud* Ingleby,
l. c., 90) and is, in my judgment, clear and expressive. In
accordance with Dr Abbott (s. 494 seq.), who has rightly
understood this metrical peculiarity, such endings might also
be called feet with two extra-syllables. I am even prepared
to submit to the reader's choice two more terms by which
to designate them: they might either be called dactylic
endings, or prosodical triplets or trioles; for just as the
musical triplet, to adopt the definition given by Webster, consists of 'three tones or notes sung or played in the time of

two', so the prosodical triplet consists of three syllables spoken in the time of two.

CCCLXXIII.

Whe stand up peerless.   Excellent falsehood.

IB., I, 1, 40.

A syllable pause line with a trochee after the pause; scan: —
We stand | up peer|less. ⌣ | Excel|lent false|hood.
Seymour needlessly proposed to read, *O excelling falsehood.*

CCCLXXIV.

Char. Lord Alexas, sweet Alexas, most any thing Alexas, almost most absolute Alexas, where's the soothsayer that you praised so to the queen?

IB., I, 2, 1 SEQQ.

Any thing, like *every thing*, frequently serves as conclusion to a succession of synonym or other nouns, enumerated without connectives and frequently assuming the character of a climax (see Mätzner, Englische Grammatik, 1ˢᵗ Ed., IIa, 153 seq.); it is, if I am allowed to borrow a simile from card-playing, the last trump, after all the rest have been played. Some examples will distinctly show what is meant. In As You Like It, II, 7, 166 we read: —
Sans teeth, sans eyes, sans taste, sans every thing.
The Taming of the Shrew, III, 2, 234 seqq.: —
She is my house,
My household stuff, my field, my barn,
My horse, my ox, my ass, my any thing.
Twelfth Night, III, 1, 161 seq.: —
Cesario, by the roses of the spring,
By maidhood, honour, truth, and every thing.

Twelfth Night, III, 4, 389, where Steevens has restored the true pointing: —

    Than lying, vainness, babbling, drunkenness,
    Or any taint of vice whose strong corruption
    Inhabits our frail blood.

Macbeth, III, 5, 18 seq. (no asyndeton): —

    Your vessels and your spells provide,
    Your charms and every thing beside.

Hamlet, IV, 7, 8 (compare my note on this line in my second (English) edition of 'Hamlet', p. 221): —

    As by your safety, greatness, wisdom, all things else,
    You mainly were stirr'd up.

Dekker and Middleton, The Honest Whore, III, 1 (The Works of Thomas Middleton, ed. Dyce, III, 65): —

    Put on thy master's best apparel, gown,
    Chain, cap, ruff, every thing.

Mucedorus, III, 3, 44 seq. (ed. Warnke and Prœscholdt): --
Here's a stir indeed, here's message, errand, banishment, and I cannot tell what.

These instances throw a vivid light not only on the passage under discussion, but also on that well-known speech of Gonzalo in The Tempest, I, 1, 69 seq., where the concluding *any thing* plainly requires the previous enumeration of several synonyms following each other without connectives, or, to say it in a word, a previous asyndetic series. This asyndetic series is supplied by Hanmer's ingenious conjecture than which nothing can be more convincing or possess a more valid claim to be admitted into the text: 'Now would I give a thousand furlongs of sea for an acre of barren ground, *ling*, heath, *broom*, furze, any thing.'

To revert to Antony and Cleopatra. After what has been shown to be the prevailing usage, no reasonable doubt can be entertained that *any thing* in the present passage is misplaced and that the two clauses *most any thing Alexas* and *most absolute Alexas* ought to change places. The poet certainly made Charmian say: 'Lord Alexas, sweet Alexas, most absolute Alexas, almost most any thing Alexas, &c.' A regular gradation is thus restored. Collier's conjecture *most sweet Alexas*, however ingenious, yet is unnecessary. *Absolute* occurs in the same sense in A. IV; sc. 14, l. 117 (*most absolute lord*, viz. Antony) and in Pericles, A. IV, Gower, l. 31 (*absolute Marina*).

CCCLXXV.

Sec. Mess. Fulvia thy wife is dead.
Ant. Where died she?
Sec. Mess. In Sicyon.

IB., I, 2, 122 SEQ.

Arrange and scan: —

Fulvia | thy wife | is dead. | Where died | she? In Si|cyon. The line has an extra syllable before the last pause; *Sicyon* is a trisyllabic feminine ending.

CCCLXXVI.

There's a great spirit gone! Thus did I desire it.

IB., I, 2, 126.

Pronounce *d'sire*. See *supra* note CCLXXIX and *infra* notes on II, 6, 22 and IV, 2, 40.

CCCLXXVII.

My idleness doth hatch. How now! Enobarbus!

IB., I, 2, 134.

Pronounce *En'barbus*, as a trisyllable. '*Enobarbus* in A. and C., says Abbott, s. 469, p. 354, has but one accent, wherever it stands in the verse.' It is used, however, as a word of four syllables and two accents in A. I, sc. 2, l. 87: —

A Ro|man thought | hath struck | him. E|nobar|bus,

and in A. II, sc. 2, l. 1: —

Good E|nobar|bus, 'tis | a wor|thy deed.

See S. Walker, Versification, 186, and compare note on Pericles, I, 2, 50.

———

CCCLXXVIII.

Cleo. Where is he?
Char.   I did not see him since.

In., I, 3, 1.

Steevens proposed to insert *now*; S. Walker (Crit. Exam., III, 294) *Madam*; Anon. *Charmian.* I take the verse to be a syllable pause line; scan: —

Where is | he? ⌐ | I did | not see | him since.

———

CCCLXXIX.

As you shall give the advice. By the fire.

In., I, 3, 68.

Pope read, *th' advices*; Steevens, *Now, by*. It is another syllable pause line; scan: —

As you | shall give | th' advice. | ∪ By | the fire.

———

CCCLXXX.

More womanly than he; hardly gave audience, or.

IB., I, 4, 7.

An Alexandrine according to Mr Fleay. In my conviction *audience*, *or* forms a trisyllabic feminine ending, just as *Ptolemy* does in the preceding line. As, however, I have little doubt that by some one or other of my readers this scansion will be disapproved as harsh, I take the opportunity of adding a few words on the score of so-called harsh scansions and contractions in general. To begin with, there is no absolute and unalterable rule to tell us which scansions are to be considered as harsh and which are not; it depends entirely on individual taste. Persons of refined taste may think lines and contractions harsh which in the familiar language of every day life pass as unobjectionable. But not only individuals living at one and the same time, also different stages in the evolution of the language differ in this respect. Who can tell whether the contemporaries of Shakespeare with respect to their notions of harshness, were in accordance with the contemporaries of Lord Tennyson? I, for one, am convinced of the contrary and so is Dr Abbott who is no mean authority on all points relative to the language and versification of Shakespeare and his times. The pronunciation and versification of the Elizabethan stage were certainly not those of the Victorian drawing-room; numberless instances prove that they were not subject to the strict rules to which they are tied to-day and agreeably to which Mr Fleay, Mr Ellis and others persist in scanning the unrestrained line of Shakespeare, although it is known to enjoy the freest possible rhythmical movement. 'Antony and Cleopatra' bears ample testimony to this fact, and it may be as well to gather from it a few more cases in point where trisyllabic words are used as dissyllables, be it either at the end of the line, before the pause, or anywhere else. I purposely select such lines as may be thought more or less harsh and may be construed into Alexandrines, omitting those that admit of no doubt. Compare, e. g., I, 3, 91 (*royalty*); I, 4, 46 (*lackeying*); I, 5, 46 (*opulent*); II, 1, 10 (*auguring*); II, 1, 33 (both *amorous* and *surfeiter*); II, 1, 43 (*enmities*); II, 2, 92 (*penitent* and *honesty*); II, 2, 96 (*ignorant*); II, 2, 122´ (*widower*); II, 2, 166 (*absolute*); II, 2, 202 (*amorous*); II, 3, 26 (*natural*); III, 1, 7 (*fugitive*); III, 10, 24 (*violate*); III, 10, 29 (*thereabouts*); III, 12, 19 (*hazarded*); III, 12, 26 (*eloquence*); III, 13, 23 (*ministers*); III, 13, 30 (*happiness*); III, 13, 36 (*emptiness*); III, 13, 63 (*Antony*); III, 13, 165 (*discandying* and *pelleted*); IV, 1, 3 (*personal*); IV, 4, 36 (*gallantly*); IV, 8, 35 (*promises*); IV, 12, 4 (*augurers*); IV, 12, 23 (*blossoming*); IV, 13, 10 (*monument*); IV, 14, 76 (*fortunate*); IV, 14, 117 (*absolute*); V, 1, 17 (*citizens* and *Antony*); V, 1, 63 (*quality*); V, 2, 23 (*reference*); V, 2, 142 (*treasurer*); V, 2, 237 (*liberty*); V, 2, 239 (*purposes*).

At a later date the works of Dryden and Pope, those great masters of versification, abound with similar contractions. The following are culled at random from Dryden: *fav'rites* (On Cromwell, st. 8); *emp'ric* (To Clarendon, 67); *spir'tual* (Absalom and Achitophel, I, 626); *med'cinally* (The Medal, 150); *rhet'ric* (Mac Flecknoe, 165); *orig'nal* (Religio Laici, 278); *Test'ments* (ib., 283)*); *diff'rence* (ib., 348); *med'c'nal*

---

*) It is a strange fact, that the editors of Dryden should have found a difficulty in scanning this line. Derrick and others omitted *and* before *cast* and Mr W. D. Christie (Dryden, &c., 2ᵈ Ed., Oxford, Clarendon Press, 1874, p. 273) attempts to make things square by accenting *Testaments* on the second syllable (*Testáments*, like *testátor*). No such thing! Scan: —

'Twere worth | both Test|'ments, and | cast in | the creed.

(Threnodia Augustalis, 111 and 170); *Presb'tery* (The Hind and the Panther, I, 233); *congl'bate* (Death of Lord Hastings, 35); *liqu'rish* (Wife of Bath, 319); *med'cinable* (Sigismonda and Guiscardo, 707).

With respect to Pope I cannot do better than by introducing a remark made by Dr Edwin A. Abbott in his Introduction (p. V) to Edwin Abbott's Concordance to the Works of Alexander Pope (London, 1875). 'Words, he says, are often abbreviated by Pope to an extent not now customary. Thus *Penny-worth* is pronounced *penn'orth* [The Basset-Table, 30; the same abbreviation occurs in Dryden's Prologue to Oedipus, 33. Compare also *ha'porth* (Life and Letters of William Bewick, ed. by Thomas Landseer. London, 1871, II, 177)]; *casuistry* is pronounced as a trisyllable [Rape of the Lock, V, 121] and *influence* as a dissyllable [Moral Essays, I, 142]. (*Sturgeón* is an exception). This abbreviation is often expressed in the spelling. Hence *confus'dly* [Rape of the Lock, V, 41]; *cov'nant*; *dev'l* as well as *devil*; *clam'rous* [Windsor Forest, 132]; *di'mond* as well as *diamond* [the same in Dryden]; *flatt'rer* (except twice); *gall'ry* [Epistle to Arbuthnot, 87]; *gen'ral* seventeen times, *general* once; *ign'rance* [Essay on Criticism, 508]; *immac'late* [Donne Versified, IV, 253]; *intemp'rate*; *int'rest*; *Marybone*; *'Pothecaries*. Though is, I believe, almost always spelt *tho'*, and *through*, *thro'*. Many of these abbreviated pronunciations are common in the Elizabethan Poets [nay, many more than these; in fact, the abbreviations in the Elizabethan Poets are numberless].'

Bunyan (The Pilgrim's Progress, 1678, p. 155) uses *Vanity* as a monosyllable (!); *Bartholomew* and *Claverhouse* occur as dissyllables (*Bartlmew* and *Claver'se*) in Percy's Folio Manuscript, II, 186 and in Whitelaw's Book of Scottish Ballads, 543a, respectively; as to the trisyllabic pronunciation of

Bartholomew see S. Walker, Versification, 186. The name of *Westmoreland* is generally spelt *Westmerland* in the old copies of Shakespeare, a spelling which is strikingly indicative of the abbreviated pronunciation of the word.

The trisyllabic feminine endings employed by Shakespeare do not always consist of a single word, but frequently of two and three words. This can hardly be a matter of surprise as even at the present day a large number of such dactyls occur in dactylic verse. In Charles Wolfe's celebrated poem 'The Burial of Sir John Moore' the following dactyls are found: *corpse to the*; *sods with our*; *sheet or in*; *spoke not a*; *face that was*; *tread o'er his*; *Lightly they'll*; *o'er his cold*; *little he'll*; *reck if they*; *let him sleep*; *Briton has*; *half of our*; *clock struck the*; *fame fresh and*. These dactyls are certainly not a wit less harsh than the trisyllabic feminine endings in Shakespeare which are objected to by English critics for their pretended harshness.

The reader may also be reminded of Lord Byron's triple rhymes in Don Juan, such as: *wishing all* (I, 31); *war again* (I, 38); *tombing all* (IV, 101); *tune it ye* (IX, 9); *gloom enough* (IX, 48); *accuse you all* (XII, 28); *talk'd about* (XII, 47); *term any* (XV, 36); and numerous others. However comically exaggerated these rhymes sometimes may be, yet they serve to show what the bent of English pronunciation is in this respect, and it cannot be doubted, that abbreviations and contractions, even such as are thought harsh now-a-days, are far less foreign to the genius of dramatic verse in Elizabeth's time than Alexandrines, which fell from Shakespeare's pen far more rarely, than English critics would make us believe.

In conclusion a few instances (out of many) of trisyllabic feminine endings that consist of two or three words may be added. Compare, e. g., A. III, sc. 1, l. 15 (before the pause): —

Acquire | too high | a fame, when him | we serve's | away.

A. IV, sc. 14, l. 80: —

Most use|ful for | thy coun|try. O, | sir, par|don me!

It is well known, however, that *pardon* is frequently pronounced as a monosyllable; see *supra* note CCXLIX. Perhaps, therefore, it would be more correct to scan: —

Most use|ful for | thy coun|try. O, | sir, pard'n | me!

A Winter's Tale, I, 2, 117 (before the pause): —

As in | a look|ing-glass, and then | to sigh, | as 'twere.

S. Walker (Crit. Exam., III, 91) needlessly conjectured *glass* for *looking-glass*, although he thinks it 'dangerous to alter without stronger reason than there appears to be in the present case.'

Richard III., I, 2, 89 (before the pause): —

Say that | I slew | them not. Why, then | they are| not dead.

Perhaps, however, this line may be taken for a 'trimeter-couplet' as well; see Abbott, s. 500. The same may be said of Troilus and Cressida, III, 3, 127 (before the pause): —

That has | he knows | not what. Nature | what things| there are,

and of Coriolanus, IV, 1, 27 (before the pause): —

As 'tis | to laugh| at 'em. My moth|er, you | wot well.

Julius Cæsar, II, 1, 285. In all old and modern editions this line is printed: —

And talk to you sometimes? Dwell I but in the suburbs.

Pope omitted *sometimes* and I once sided with him (Anglia, I, 347). 'The true prosodical view of this line, says Craik

4

(The English of Shakespeare, &c. 5th Ed., London, 1875, p. 174) is to regard the two combinations "to you" and "in the" as counting each for a single syllable. It is no more an Alexandrine than it is an hexameter.' Although the same scansion is given by S. Walker (Crit. Exam., I, 221), yet I am unable to acquiesce in it. It now seems to me that *sometimes* has slipped out of its place and should be transposed, and that *talk to you* is a trisyllabic feminine ending before the pause:—

> And some|times talk | t' you? Dwell I | but in | the sub|urbs.

———

CCCLXXXI.

So much as lank'd not.

   Lep.   'Tis pity of him.

   Cæs. Let his shames quickly

Drive him to Rome: 'tis time we twain

Did show, ourselves i' the field.

Ib., I, 4, 71 seqq.

Arrange (with Mr Fleay) and scan:—

> So much | as lank'd | not. 'Tis pit|y of him. | Let's shames
> Quickly | drive him | to Rome. | 'Tis time | we twain.
> Did show ourselves i' th' field.

Let's = let his; compare III, 7, 12: *from's time*; Twelfth Night, III, 4, 326: *for's oath sake.* Mr Fleay, of course, declares l. 71 to be an Alexandrine with the cesura at the ninth syllable:—

> So much as lankt not. || 'Tis pity of him. | Let his shames.

I wonder, how he scans this so-called Alexandrine.

———

CCCLXXXII.

Once name you derogately, when to sound your name.

IB., II, 2, 34.

This line is not mentioned by Mr Fleay; in my judgment
it is to be scanned: —

Once name | you der|'gately, | when t' sound | your name.

CCCLXXXIII.

Eno. Go to, then; your considerate stone.

IB., II, 2, 112.

Read either: —

    Go to, then, *you* considerate stone,

or: —

    Go to, | then; ‿ | *you're a* | consid|erate stone,

or: —

    Go to, | then; *you* | *are a* | consid|erate stone.

The meaning is: You are indeed considerate (= discreet,
circumspect), but at the same time 'senseless as a stone',
inaccessible to conciliatory and tender emotions.

CCCLXXXIV.

Would then be nothing: truths would be tales.

IB., II, 2, 137.

A syllable pause line; scan: —

Would then | be noth|ing: ‿ | truths would | be tales.

All conjectures are needless; the best of them is that by
Staunton: *half tales.*

---

4 *

CCCLXXXV.

By duty ruminated.

    Ant.   Will Cæsar speak?

    Cæs. Not till he hears how Antony is touch'd
With what is spoke already.

    Ant.   What power is in Agrippa.

IB., II, 2, 141 SEQQ.

Already, in l. 143, is omitted by Hanmer. Arrange and scan:—

By du|ty rum|'natèd. |

    Ant.   Will Cæ|sar speak?

    Cæs. Not till | he hears | how An|tony is touch'd | with what
- Is spoke | 'alread|y.

    Ant.   What power | is in | Agrip|pa.

Antony is is to be pronounced as a dissyllable (= *Ant'ny's*);
compare III, 3, 44 (*creature's*); III, 7, 70 (*leader's*); &c. Thus
the Alexandrine is got rid of.

CCCLXXXVI.

Her people out upon her; and Antony.

IB., II, 2, 219.

Scan either:—

Her peo|ple out | upon | her. And An|tony,

or (as a syllable pause line with a trisyllabic feminine ending):—

Her peo|ple out | upon | her; — | and An|tony.

CCCLXXXVII.

Whom ne'er the word of 'No' woman heard speak.

IB., II, 2, 228.

Capell's conjecture (*never the word — no*) does not improve the line; the only means to render it smoother would be by a transposition: —
Whom *woman* ne'er the word of 'No' heard speak.

CCCLXXXVIII.

Her infinite variety: other women cloy
The appetites they feed, but she makes hungry.

IB., II, 2, 241 SEQ.

Arrange: —
Her infinite variety: other women
Cloy th' appetites they feed, but she makes hungry.
Variety is, of course, to be read as a trisyllable. Another Alexandrine is thus done away with.

CCCLXXXIX.

There saw you labouring for him. What was't.

IB., II, 6, 14.

This line may be differently scanned; either: —
There saw | you la|bouring | for him. | What was't.
or: —
There saw | you la|b'ring for | him. ⏒ | What was't.
To me this latter scansion seems preferable.

CCCXC.

To scourge the ingratitude that despiteful Rome.

IB., II, 6, 22.

Scan: —
To scourge | th' ingrat|itude | of d'spite|ful Rome.
For the pronunciation *d'spiteful* see note on I, 2, 126.

CCCXCI.

Then so much have I heard.

IB., II, 6, 68.

A mutilated line; add: *Mark Antony*: —

Then so much have I heard, *Mark Antony.*

———

CCCXCII.

It nothing ill becomes thee.

IB., II, 6, 81.

Another defective line, to be completed by the addition of *Enobarbus*: —

It nothing ill becomes thee, *Enobarbus.*

———

CCCXCIII.

And, as I said before, that which is the strength of their amity shall prove the immediate author of their variance.

IB., II, 6, 136 SEQQ.

The context clearly shows that the poet did not write, *the strength of their* AMITY, but, *the strength of their* UNITY, referring the words not to l. 130: *the very strangler of their amity,* but to l. 122 seqq.: *Then is Cæsar and he for ever knit together.* Eno. *If I were bound to divine of their unity, I would not prophesy so. Variance,* in l. 138, is not a suitable antithesis to *amity,* but it is to *unity.*

———

CCCXCIV.

These drums! these trumpets, flutes! what!

IB., II, 7, 138.

A badly mutilated line which is far from being restored by
Hanmer's omission of *flutes*. Qy. read: —

These drums! | these trum|pets! $\smile$ | *these* flutes! | what *ho*!?

That the exclamation *ho!* originally formed part of Menas's
speech and most probably of this very line results from the
words of Enobarbus: *Ho! says a'. There's my cap!*, to which
Menas replies: *Ho! noble captain, come.*

―――

CCCXCV.

And in his offence
Should my performance perish.
Sil.   Thou hast, Ventidius, that.
IB., III, 1, 26 SEQ.

Qy. omit *Ventidius?*

―――

CCCXCVI.

This creature's no such thing.
Char.   Nothing, madam.
IB., III, 3, 44.

A syllable pause line; scan: —

This crea|ture's no | such thing. | ∪ Noth|ing, mad|am.

Pope's and Keightley's conjectures are unnecessary.

―――

CCCXCVII.

Cæs. Most certain. Sister, welcome: pray you,
Be ever known to patience: my dear'st sister!
IB., III, 6, 97 SEQ.

Arrange and read: —

Cæs. Most certain. Sister, welcome: pray you, *be*
E'er known | to pa|tience: $\smile$ | my *dear|est* sis|ter;

or: —

E'er known | to pa|ti-ence: | my dear|est sis|ter.
Compare Abbott, s. 510 (p. 419).

———

CCCXCVIII.

Hoists sails and flies.
Eno. That I beheld.

IB., III, 10, 15 SEQ.

A complete blankverse may be restored by the insertion of
Enobarbus : —

Hoists sails | and flies, | *Enobar*|*bus.*
　Eno.　　　　　　　　　That I | beheld.

For the trisyllabic pronunciation of *Enobarbus* see note on
I, 2, 134. According to the Cambridge Edition Capell proposed *sail* for *sails*; compare, however, the concluding song
in Westward Ho! (Webster, ed. Dyce, 1857, in 1 vol.,
p. 245 b): —

Hoist up sails, and let's away.

———

CCCXCIX.

Why then good night indeed.

IB., III, 10, 30.

Another defective line; read: —
Why then good night indeed, *Canidius.*

———

CD.

Which leaves itself: to the sea-side straightway.

IB., III, 11, 20.

A syllable pause line; scan: —
Which leaves | itself: | ∪ to | the sea-|side straight|way.

———

CDI.
Frighted each other, why should he follow?

IB., III, 13, 6.

The attempts made by Pope and an anonymous critic to correct this seemingly corrupt verse are needless; it is a syllable pause line and thus to be scanned: —

Frighted | each oth|er, ⊥ | why should | he fol|low?

CDII.
Hear it apart.

Cleo.   None but friends: say boldly.

IB., III, 13, 47.

A syllable pause line again; scan: —

Hear | it apart. |

Cleo.   ᴜ None | but friends: | say bold|ly.

All conjectures on this line recorded in the Cambridge Edition are needless.

CDIII.
Your Cæsar's father oft
When he hath mused of taking kingdoms in.

IB., III, 13, 82 SEQ.

Arrange: —

Your Cæsar's father
Oft, when he hath mused of taking kingdoms in.

He hath is to be contracted into one syllable; compare IV, 1, 3 (*He hath whipped*); IV, 15, 14:

(*Not Cæ|sar's val|our hath o'er|thrown An|tony,*

unless the pause after *valour* be deemed of sufficient strength to admit of an extra syllable); Twelfth Night, V, 1, 372

(*he hath married her*); Pericles, I, 1, 143 (*He hath found*);
ib., II, 1, 132 (*it hath been a shield*). — Another Alexandrine is thus eliminated.

———

CDIV.

Authority melts from me: of late, when I cried 'Ho!'
Like boys unto a muss, kings would start forth,
And cry 'Your will?' Have you no ears?
I am Antony yet. Take hence this Jack and whip him.
IB., III, 13, 90 SEQQ.

With respect to the division of these lines I completely agree
with Hanmer, whose arrangement is as follows: —

Authority melts from me: of late, when I
Cried 'Ho!' like boys unto a muss, kings would
Start forth, and cry 'Your will?' Have you no ears?
I'm Antony yet. Take hence this Jack and whip him.

———

CDV.

Laugh at his challenge. Cæsar must think.
IB., IV, 1, 6.

All attempts at completing this line recorded in the Cambridge Edition are needless; scan: —

Laugh at | his chal|lenge. ⏌ | Cæsar | must think.

———

CDVI.

For I spake to you for your comfort; did desire you.
IB., IV, 2, 40.

'In IV, 2, 40,' says Mr Fleay, who declares the line to be an
Alexandrine, 'cesura after ninth syllable'. In my opinion
we have to deal with a regular blankverse; scan: —

For I | spake to | you for | your com|fort; did d'sire | you.

The line has an extra syllable before the pause. For the
monosyllabic pronunciation of *desire* see note on I, 2, 126.

CDVII.

Char. Please you, retire to your chamber.
Cleo.   ·   Lead me.

IB., IV, 4, 35.

An unmetrical and defective line, unless recourse be had to
the prolongation of *retire*: —

Please you, | reti|ire to | your cham|ber. Lead | me.

Compare Abbott, s. 480. Rowe (2ᵈ Ed.) added *to* before
retire, Seymour *you* after it. A third way of completing the
line would be by the insertion of *madam*: —

Please you, | retire | t' your cham|ber, *mad*|*am*. Lead | me.

CDVIII.

Eros.   Sir, his chests and treasure
He has not with him.
Ant.   Is he gone?
Sold.   Most certain.

IB., IV, 5, 10 SEQ.

The words *Most certain* are erroneously ascribed to the Soldier; they belong to Eros. The Soldier has already informed
Antony that Enobarbus *is with Cæsar*, but Antony, unwilling
to believe him, appeals to the higher authority of Eros,
asking him whether Enobarbus be really gone (*Is he gone?*)
and is answered by Eros, *Most certain*.

CDIX.

Make it so known.

 Agr. Cæsar, I shall.

IB., IV, 6, 3.

Not two short lines, as printed in the Cambridge and Globe Editions, by Dyce, Delius; &c., but a defective blankverse which is to be completed by the addition of *Agrippa:* —

 Make it | so known, | *Agrip*|*pa*. Cæsar, | I shall.

CDX.

I tell you true: best you safed the bringer.

IB., IV, 6, 26.

A syllable pause line; scan: —

 I tell | you true: | ∪ best | you safed | the bring|er.

All conjectures (see Cambridge Edition) may be dispensed with.

CDXI.

Each man's like mine: you have shown all Hectors.

IB., IV, 8, 7.

Another syllable pause line; scan: —

 Each man's | like mine: | ∪ you | have shown | all Hect|ors.

S. Walker's and the anonymous critic's conjectures recorded in the Cambridge Edition are needless.

CDXII.

He has deserved it, were it carbuncled.

IB., IV, 8, 28.

This too is a syllable pause line: —

 He has | deserved | it, ⌐ | were it | carbun|cled.

Or would it be more correct to scan:

 He has | deser|vèd it, | were it | carbun|cled?

CDXIII.

Make mingle. with our. rattling. tabourines. ..

IB., IV, 8, 37.

After· this. verse a line has evidently been, lost. in, which those sounds were. mentioned, that heaven 'strikes, together,' with the sounds. of the earth, the trumpets and rattling tabourines.

.... O   CDXIV.

O ·Antony l O Antony!

    Sec.· Sold.   Let's speak

To ·him. ·

    First Sold. Let's hear him, for the things he speaks May concern Cæsar.

IB., IV, 9, 23 SEQQ.

Qy. read, arrange, and scan: —

O An|tony l | O An|t'ny!

    Sec. Sold.   Let's speak | to him.

    First Sold. *Nay,* let | *us* hear | him, for | the things |

                           he speaks

May con|cern Cæ|sar?

Capell inserted *further* after *hear, him.* Compare note on Cymbeline, V, 5, 238.

CDXV.

Hark! the drums Demurely wake the sleepers.

IB.; IV, 9, 31.

Perhaps *Do yarely* instead of *Demurely* which cannot possibly be right.

CDXVI.

I learn'd of thee. How! not dead? not dead?

IB., IV, 14, 103.

There is no need of Pope's conjecture, *not* YET *dead.* Scan:—

I learn'd | of thee. | ᴗ How! | not dead? | not dead?

CDXVII.

His guard have brought him hither. O sun.

IB., IV, 15, 9.

Here too there is no need of filling up the line as has been done by Pope's and Capell's conjectures (*O* THOU *sun* and *O sun,* SUN). Scan:—

His guard | have brought | him hith|er. ⏉ | O sun!

CDXVIII.

I lay upon thy lips.

　　Cleo.　　　　I dare not, dear, —

Dear my lord, pardon, — I dare not.

IB., IV, 15, 21 SEQ.

Read and arrange:—

I lay upon thy lips. *Come down.*

　　Cleo.　　　　　　　　I dare not,

Dear, dear my lord, pardon, — I dare not *come.*

Come down, in l. 21, has been added most happily by Theobald; the context shows that it cannot be dispensed with. For *come,* in l. 22, I must answer myself; without this addition the line would have to be scanned:—

　　Dear, dear | my lord, | ᴗ par|don, — I | dare not,

a scansion which will hardly receive the approval of competent critics.

CDXIX.

Splitted the heart. This is his sword.

IB., V, 1, 24.

According to the Cambridge Edition Hanmer added *itself* after *heart*; Collier's MS. corrector: *Split that self noble heart.* If the line is to be filled up, it would seem more probable that the name of the person addressed was lost and should be inserted: —

Splitted the heart. *Cæsar,* this is his sword.

Or we might read: —

Splitted *that very* heart. This is his sword.

After all, however, I think the line should be left as it stands, since verses of four feet are pretty frequent when there is a break in the line or a change of thought; see Abbott, s. 507.

CDXX.

The gods rebuke me, but it is tidings.

IB., V, 1, 27.

Rowe, *a Tiding.* There is, however, no need of correction; it is a syllable pause line: —

The gods | rebuke | me, ⌣ | but it | is ti|dings.

CDXXI.

His voice was propertied
As all the tuned spheres, and that to friends;
But when he meant to quail and shake the orb,
He was as rattling thunder.

IB., V, 2, 83 SEQQ.

Instead of *and that to friends,* Theobald reads: WHEN *that to friends,* and an anonymous critic (the Cambridge Editors?)

proposes, ADDRESS *to friends*. I think we should read either, *and* SOFT *to friends* or, *and* SWEET *to friends*; *low* would not come near enough to the *ductus literarum*. Antony's voice when speaking to friends is forcibly contrasted to the 'rattling thunder' to which it is likened when he is speaking to foes. Shakespeare repeatedly praises a low voice in woman; of Cordelia her father says (V, 3, 272 seq.): —

Her voice was ever soft,
Gentle, and low, an excellent thing in woman.

May not what is an excellent thing in woman, be an excellent thing in Antony too, when he is speaking to his friends?

CDXXII.

What should I stay — _ _ _ _
Char. In this vile world? So, fare thee well.
IB., V, 2, 316 SEQ.

The words: *In this vile world* do not belong to Charmian, but to Cleopatra who already before (IV, 15, 60 seq.) has complained of 'this dull world' which, she says, in Antony's absence is 'no better than a sty.' Arrange, therefore: —

What should I stay in this vile world —
Char.   So, fare thee well.

Shakespeare certainly wrote *vilde*, not *wilde*. *Fare thee well* would appear to be a trisyllabic feminine ending.*)

---

*) These notes on 'Antony and Cleopatra' (CCCLXXII—CDXXII) were first published in Prof. Kölbing's *Englische Studien*, Vol. IX, p. 267—278. Like, the notes on 'Cymbeline' and 'Pericles' they have since been revised and corrected.

CDXXIII.

Unto a poor but worthy gentleman: she's wedded;
Her husband banished; she imprison'd: all
Is outward sorrow; though I think the king
Be touch'd at very heart.

Sec. Gent. None but the king?

CYMBELINE, I, I, 7 SEQQ.

This is the arrangement of the Folios; it is quite correct and
all conjectures to which the passage has given rise are gratuitous; nor is Mr Fleay right in declaring l. 7 to be one
of six feet. *Gentleman* may be read either as a trisyllable,
or as a dissyllable (see S. Walker, Versification, 189 seq.); in
the former case we have a trisyllabic feminine ending, in the
latter an extra syllable, before the pause.*)

—————

*) The above notes on Cymbeline (CDXXIII — DXXIX) were
first printed in Professor Wülker's Anglia, Vol. VIII, p. 263 — 297,
and were embodied in a Letter to C. M. Ingleby, Esq., M. A., LL. D.,
V. P. R. S. L. The introductory words of this Letter which I hope
I shall be allowed to reproduce, were to the following effect: 'Dear
Ingleby! When, in October last, at the beginning of our winter-
term, I entered upon a course of lectures on Shakespeare's 'Cymbeline', I was surprised by the unexpected news that you were
engaged in preparing a new edition of this most attractive, though
at the same time most thorny play. You will easily believe that
under these circumstances my thoughts turned to you whenever I
was beset by one of those perplexing difficulties both critical and
exegetical with which this play abounds. It was natural that I should
have wished to talk such passages over with you in your genial
study at Valentines and thus to clear away *viribus unitis* some of
those *cruces interpretum*. This privilege, however, was denied me,
and a continued correspondence on the subject of our studies would
have been too heavy a task not only on your time, but also on
mine. The next best thing, therefore, I can do, is to lay before you

5

CDXXIV.

Of the king's looks, hath a heart that is not.

IB., I, I, 14.

S. Walker, according to the Cambridge Edition, suspects a corruption here. The line would indeed be intolerably harsh, if scanned: —

Of the | king's looks, | hath a | heart that | is not.

In my opinion, however, there is no need of correction, the verse being either a syllable pause line: —

Of the | king's looks, | ᴗ hath | a heart | that is | not,

or *Of* taking the place of a monosyllabic foot: —

Of | the king's | looks, hath | a heart | that is | not.

―――――

CDXXV.

To his protection, calls him Posthumus Leonatus.

IB., I, I, 41.

Neither of the two names can be dispensed with, both of them being required by the context. The correct explanation of the line has been given by Dyce and Staunton *ad loc.* 'Various passages in these plays, says Dyce, show that Shakespeare (like his contemporary dramatists) occasionally

―――――

in print all those notes and conjectural emendations that have presented themselves to me in the course of my lectures. As your edition has been unavoidably postponed they may still prove serviceable to you in the revision and explanation of the badly corrupted text; your friendly disposition towards me will no doubt prompt you to gather from them all the critical honey they may contain and to favour me with your opinion of what you approve and of what you disapprove. Here, then, they are.'

disregarded metre when proper names were to be introduced.'
He then refers his readers to his note on 2 K. Henry VI,
I, 1, 7: —

The Dukes of Orleans, Calaber, Bretagne, and Alençon.

'I may observe, he says there, that Shakespeare has allowed
this line to stand just as he found it in The First Part of
the Contention, &c.; and; indeed, even in the plays which
are wholly his own, he, like other early dramatists, considered
himself at liberty occasionally to disregard the laws of metre
in the case of proper names: e. g., a blankverse speech in
Richard II, Act II, sc. 1 contains the following formidable
line: —

'Sir John Norbery, Sir Robert Waterton, and Francis
Quoint.'

To this instance Dyce, in his second edition, has added
three similar lines, but has been singularly unfortunate in
their choice, as they can be scanned without the least correction or difficulty. The first of them is taken from The
Two Gentlemen of Verona, II, 4, 54, and is to be scanned
in the following manner: —

Know | ye Don | Anto|nio, your coun|tryman?

The line begins with a monosyllabic foot and has an extra
syllable before the pause. The second line is from A. V,
sc. 1 of the same play and its only irregularity is an extra-
syllable before the pause: —

That Sil|via, at Fri|ar Pat|rick's cell, | should meet | me.

The third instance, also from the same comedy (V, 2, 34),
may certainly be considered as one line, as printed by Dyce,
in which case *Valentine* is to be read as a trisyllabic feminine
ending; there is, however, no occasion to depart from the

arrangement of the first Folio, which, amongst others, has
been adopted by the Cambridge and Globe Editors: —
      Duke. Why then,
She's fled unto that peasant Valentine.
Even the 'formidable' and most likely corrupt passage in
Richard II, II, 1, 281 seqq. might perhaps be satisfactorily
regulated in this way: —
    That late | broke from | the Duke | of Ex|eter,
    His broth|er, Archbish|op late | of Can|terbur|y,
    Sir Thom|as Er|pingham | *and* Sir |John Ram|ston,
    Sir | John Nor|bery, ..
    Sir Rob|ert Wa|terton | and Fran|cis Quoint.
Should S. Walker, Versification, 100, be right in maintaining
that *Archbishop* is generally accented on the first syllable, a
slight transposition of the word will meet the requirements
of the case: —
    His broth|er, late Arch|bishop | of Can|terbur|y.
    To revert to 'Cymbeline'. Staunton's note on the line in
question is to the following effect: 'The old poets not unfrequently introduce proper names without regard to the measure.' To this he adds another remark of no little import;
'occasionally indeed, he says, as if at the discretion of the
player, the name was to be spoken or not.' The truth, in
my opinion, is, that the names of the interlocutors as well as
words of address seem frequently either to have been wrongly
left out or wrongly added by the carelessness of the players
and copyists, especially at the end of the line. Indeed a
great number of verses may be corrected either by the
addition, or (though less frequently) by the omission of the
name of the person addressed. See my note on Hamlet
(second edition), s. 59 (Reynaldo); note XLV, &c.

CDXXVI.

Could make him the receiver of; which he took.

IB., I, 1, 44.

Scan: —

Could make | him the | recei'er | of; which | he took.

See Abbott, s. 166. Compare also l. 72 of this very scene: —
Evil [E'il] - eyed | unto | you: you're. | my pris|'ner, but,
wrongly altered by Pope to Ill-eyed &c. See S. Walker,
Crit. Exam., II, 196.

CDXXVII.

As we do air, fast as 'twas minister'd,
And in 's spring became a harvest, lived in court.

IB., I, 1, 45 SEQ.

Both Mr Fleay and Mr Ellis (On Early English Pronunciation,
III, 946) register l. 46 among what they are pleased to call
Alexandrines. Hertzberg (*Shakespeare's Dramatische Werke
nach der Übersetzung von Schlegel und Tieck, herausgegeben
durch die Deutsche Shakespeare-Gesellschaft,* XII, 453) likewise thinks that it would be the easiest expedient to read
And in his spring &c. and thus to make the line one of those
Alexandrines, of which, he says, there is no want in Cymbeline. In my conviction Capell has come nearest to the truth
by adding *And* to the preceding line; only he should not
have dissolved *in's.* Arrange and read accordingly: —

As we do air, fast as 'twas minister'd, and
In's spring became a harvest, lived in court, &c.

Minister'd is, of course, to be pronounced as a dissyllable
(*min'ster'd*); see Abbott, s. 468.

CDXXVIII.

A sample, to, the youngest, to the more mature.

IB., I, 1, 48.

Mr Fleay has no doubt that this is an Alexandrine, and I
have no doubt that it is not. *Youngest* is either to be pronounced as a monosyllable, like *eldest* ten lines *infra*; or, if
the dissyllabic pronunciation should be preferred, it contains
an extra-syllable before the pause. The article before *more*
is to be elided (or read as a proclitic) just as it is the case
eight lines lower down: *to th' king*, and l. 59: *I' th' swathing-
clothes*. Scan, therefore, either: —

A sam|ple to | the young'st, | to th' more | mature,

or: —

A sam|ple to | the young|est, to th' more | mature.

CDXXIX.

I' th' swathing-clothes the other, from their nursery.

IB., I, 1, 59.

No Alexandrine, *nursery* being a trisyllabic feminine ending.
Compare the scansion of *imagery* in Spenser's Faerie Queene,
VII, 7, 10: —

That richer seem'd than any tapestry,
That Princes bowres adorne with painted imagery.

CDXXX.

That could not trace them!
First Gent.   Howsoe'er 'tis strange.

IB., I, 1, 65.

Qy. THAT'T or THAT' *could not trace them?* Compare III,
4, 80: *That* [qy. THAT'T?] *cravens my weak hand.* See
S. Walker, Versification, 77 seqq.

CDXXXI.

I will be known your advocate: 'marry, yet.'

IB., I, 1, 76.

S. Walker, Versification, 187, endeavours to show that *marry* 'is commonly a monosyllable' and that it 'would have been irregular' to scan: —

I will | be known | your ad|v'cate; mar|ry yet.

Nevertheless I own that I prefer this scansion, so much the more as S. Walker has not succeeded in proving his case. Apart from a line in Hudibras (III, 3, 644), in which the *y* of *Marry* is to be contracted with the following *hang*, he only instances K. Richard III, III, 4, 58, where *marry* may just as well be read as a trochee and *he is* may be contracted: —

Marry, | that with | no man | here he's | offend|ed.

If some reader or other should object that by this scansion *no* is placed in the unaccented, instead of the accented part of the measure, he may be referred to note CVIII (Vol. II, p. 8 seqq.). In support of his theory S. Walker also adduces *sirrah*, which, he says, is 'frequently at least' pronounced as a monosyllable, e. g., 3 K. Henry VI, V, 6, 6. But may not this line be read and scanned: —

Sirrah, | leave's to | ourselves: | we must | confer?

In conclusion the reader's attention may be called to the fact that in all the lines quoted, a pause follows after both *marry* and *sirrah* which would seem to speak in favour of my scansions. That in the line quoted from Hudibras the pause does not impede the contraction of the two vowels, cannot be a matter of surprise.

CDXXXII.

Imo. O blest, that I might not! I chose an eagle,
And did avoid a puttock.

Ib., I, 1, 139 seq.

'A puttock, says Singer *ad. loc.*, is a mean degenerate species
of hawk, too worthless to deserve training.' This 'note
re-appears in the Rev. H. Hudson's edition in a slightly
altered shape: 'A puttock, he says, is a mean degenerate
hawk, not worth training.' Delius has nothing better to say;
his note is to the following effect: '*Puttock, ein Habicht schlechter*
Art.' What does a. 'degenerate hawk' mean? I am unable
to attach a meaning to this phrase. The fact is that the
puttock does not belong to the *falcones nobiles*, as they are
termed in natural history, but is a species of kite *(Milvus*
ictinus, the glede). According to Naumann und Gräfe, *Hand-*
buch der Naturgeschichte der drei Reiche &c. (Eisleben und
Leipzig, 1836) I, 362 the *Milvi* are '*von traurigem Ansehn,*
träge und feig, und können den Raub nicht fliegend ergreifen,
sondern nur sitzende und kriechende Thiere fangen, und fressen
auch Aas.' '*Der rothe Milan (Gabelweihe, Königsweihe, Falco*
Milvus), the same authors continue, *jagt junge Hühner, Enten,*
Gänse und andere junge oder des Flugvermögens beraubte
Vögel, Mäuse, Maulwürfe, Amphibien, indem er niedrig über
den Boden wegstreicht, fällt gern auf Aas.' The chief point,
as I take it, is that the *Milvi* are incapable of catching birds
on the wing, but only when sitting or walking about. This
is the reason why they were held in disregard by all lovers
of hawking and why all attempts at training cannot but be
lost on them, since training may improve, but cannot alter
the natural gifts of bird or beast. Thus the name of 'puttock' passed into a by-word and an expression of contempt.
The derivation of the word serves as an eloquent confirmation

of this theory, *puttock* being by no means a diminutive, but a corruption of *poot-hawk*, i. e. a hawk that preys on poots or pouts; *pout*, as Prof. Skeat has shown, standing for *poult* = *pullet* (Fr. *poulet*) from Lat. *pullus*.

CDXXXIII.

Leave us to ourselves; and make yourself some comfort.

IB., I, 1, 155.

Scan either: —

Leave us | t' ourselves; | and make | yourself | some com|fort, or, which I think preferable: —

Leave's to | ourselves; | and make | yourself | some com|fort.

CDXXXIV.

Queen.   Fie, you must give way.

IB., I, 1, 158.

This is the punctuation of all the Ff. Modern editors punctuate either: Fie! you must &c., or: Fie! — you must &c., thus awakening the belief, as if in their opinion the words were addressed to two different persons. Not content with such an indirect hint, Delius explicitly refers the interjection *Fie!* to the preceding speech of Cymbeline, whereas he declares only the rest of the words to be addressed to Imogen. I cannot subscribe to such a division of the Queen's admonition. On hearing her father's terrible malediction Imogen very naturally gives expression to her wounded feelings by some gesture of impatience and horror and is reproved by her stepmother rather energetically, as only in l. 153 she has been desired to keep quiet (*Peace, Dear lady daughter, peace!*). She does not utter her grief and dismay in words, but her

continued gesticulation shows that her mother's first injunction
has been of little avail and requires repetition. The only
words addressed to the King by the Queen are in l. 153:
Beseech your patience.

CDXXXV.

Pray you speake with me;
You shall (at least) &c.

Ib., I, 1, 177.

This is the arrangement and reading of the Ff. Almost all
editors since Capell have adopted his suggestion to add *I*
before *pray*, which, they say, has been lost. Nevertheless it
may be submitted that the line is quite correct, if scanned
as a syllable pause line: — — —

Pray you, | ∪ speak | with me: | you shall | at least.

I adopt, of course, the arrangement of the lines as proposed
by Capell and think the Ff as well as Rowe faulty in this
respect.

CDXXXVI.

Clo. You'll go with us?
First Lord. I'll attend your lordship.
Clo. Nay, come, let's go together.
Sec. Lord. Well, my lord.

Ib., I, 2, 40 seqq.

Capell, Dyce, and the Rev. H. Hudson have assigned the
words: '*I'll attend your lordship*' to the Second Lord. Delius,
on the other hand, suspects that the concluding speech:
Well, my lord, should be given to the First Lord. In my
conviction both parties are wrong. In reply to Cloten's
invitation, addressed to the two lords conjointly, to accom-

pany him to his chamber, the First Lord who is a flatterer
and a flunkey, at once declares himself ready to attend his
lordship; the second, however, who knows and dislikes his
master thoroughly, either offers to stay behind, or to leave
the stage by a different door, but is prevented from doing
so by Cloten's reiterated summons: *Nay, come, let's go
together*, to which he cannot but reply in the affirmative:
Well, my lord. Only on the stage the correctness of this
explanation can be made fully apparent. Compare note on
II, 1, 48.

CDXXXVII.

Imo. Then waved his handkerchief?
Pis.   And kiss'd it, madam.
Imo. Senseless linen! happier therein than I!
And that was all?
  Pis.   No, madam, for so long &c.
Iв., I, 3, 6 SEQQ.

This is the arrangement of the folios. Line 7 is thus to be
scanned: —
    Sense|less lin|en! Happier | therein | than I,
a scansion which exhibits indeed three deviations from the
normal type, viz. a monosyllabic foot, an extra syllable before
the pause, and a trochee after it. The scansion given by
Dr Abbott, s. 453: —
    Senseless | linen! | Happier | therein | than I
looks very plausible at first sight, but on second thoughts
appears too abnormal to find assent; it contains no less than
three consecutive trochees! S. Walker, Crit. Exam., III, 316,
would arrange as follows: —
    Imo. Then waved his handkerchief?
    Pis. And kiss'd it, madam.

Imo.   Senseless linen, happier
Therein than I!!
And that was all?
Pis.   No, madam; for so long &c.

If, however, the division of the old copies is to be departed
from, the following arrangement seems preferable:—

Imo. Then waved his handkerchief?
Pis.   And kiss'd it, madam.
Imo. Senseless linen!
Happier therein than I! And that was all?
Pis. No, madam; for so long
As he could make &c.

_____

CDXXXVIII.

When shall we hear from him? Be assured, madam.

IB., I, 3, 23.

Scan:—

" When shall | we hear | from him? | Be assur'ed, mad|am.

I shall disbelieve the pretended accentuation *maddm*, until
convinced by a case, where *mádam* is simply impossible. The
very next passage on which I shall comment is a case in
point, in so far as here the poet would seem to have accented
the word on the last syllable, but has not. This passage is:—

_____

CDXXXIX.

Shakes all our buds from growing.
          Enter a Lady.
Lady.   The queen, madam.
Desires your highness' company.

IB., I, 3, 37 SEQ.

The first line admits of a twofold scansion, either: —

Shakes all | our buds | from grow|ing. The queen, | madám, or : —

Shakes all | our buds | from grow|ing. The | queen, mad|am.

But what, if neither of these two scansions should have been the poet's own? The above arrangement of the Ff has indeed been retained by all editors, as far as I know; however, the words spoken by the Lady form a complete blankverse by themselves and the passage should be divided accordingly: —

Shakes all our buds from growing.

Enter a Lady.

Lady. The queen, | madam, | desires | your high|ness
        com|pany.

Need I add, that *madam*, although in the second place, is a trochee (compare Abbott, s. 453 and my second edition of 'Hamlet', s. 118), and *company* a trisyllabic feminine ending? By this division the incomplete line is shifted from the speech of the Lady which it does not fit at all, to that of Imogen where it finds a far more appropriate place. As to *madam* Mr Fleay, in his edition of Marlowe's 'Edward II.,' p. 120, thinks it a strong argument in favour of the accentuation *madám*, that the old texts write *Madame* which spelling, in his opinion, is plainly indicative of the French accentuation of the word. In the present passage, however, as well as in I, 1, 23, the Ff uniformly write *Madam*, whilst in other passages (e. g. in Love's Labour's Lost, V, 2, 431) we read *Madame*, although the word be undoubtedly accented on the first syllable. Compare *supra* note CCLXIX. — In order to prevent a mistaken scansion one more line may be added, viz. A. I, sc. 5, l. 5: —

Pleaseth | your high|ness, ay: | here they | are, mad|am.

CDXL.

But, though slow, deadly.

 . *Queen.*   I wonder, doctor.

              IB., I, 5, 10.

Theobald and, independently of him, S. Walker, Versification, 24: I *do* wonder. There is, however, no need of such
an insertion, the verse being a syllable pause line; scan:—

 But, though | slow, dead|ly. ⊥ | I won|der, doc|tor.

Or should we come still nearer to the poet's own scansion
by reading *But* as a monosyllabic foot:—

 But, | though slow, | deadly. | I won|der doc|tor?

CDXLI.

Think on my words. [*Exeunt Queen and Ladies.*

 . *Pis.*   And shall do.

              IB., I, 5, 85.

According to the Cambridge Edition Steevens suspects an
omission here. Singer adds the following note: 'Some words,
which rendered this sentence less abrupt, and perfected the
metre, appear to have been omitted in the old copies.' Add
gracious madam after *shall do*, and all will be right:—

 Think on | my words. |

      And shall | do, gra|cious mad|am.

Compare note on I, 1, 41.

CDXLII.

What are men mad? Hath nature given them eyes
· To see this vaulted arch, and the rich crop
Of sea and land, which can distinguish 'twixt

The fiery orbs above and the twinned stones
Upon the number'd beach? and can we not
Partition make with spectacles so precious
'Twixt fair and foul?

IB., I, 6, 32 SEQQ.

Instead of *the number'd* Theobald reads rightly: *th' unnumber'd.*
Compare K. Lear, IV, 6, 20 seqq.: —

the murmuring surge
That on the unnumbered idle pebbles chafes,
Cannot be heard so high.

The *'crop of sea and land'* undoubtedly means the crop of
the sea on the land, or the crop on the margin between
the sea and land, i. e. that profusion of pebbles, shells, sea-
weeds, &c. that are washed on shore by the waves and con-
stitute, so to say, the harvest which the land reaps from the
ocean. The poet places side by side those two natural phe-
nomena where an innumerable abundance of similar, nay
almost undistinguishable (I beg pardon for coining the word)
objects are gathered together: the firmament with its myriads
of stars and the unnumbered beach with its pebbles that are
as like to each other as twins. Now, he continues, if men's
eyes are capable of distinguishing some individual star or
pebble from its twin, can they not, on beholding the divine
form of Imogen, make partition between fair and foul, between
an untainted virtuous lady and one of the common sort,
persons that even in their outward appearance are so wide
apart?

CDXLIII.

An eminent monsieur, that, it seems, much loves.

IB., I, 6, 65.

Scan: —

An em|'nent mon|sieur, that, | it seems, | much loves.
Compare Love's Labour's Lost, II, 1, 196: —

A gal|lant la|dy. Mon|sieur, fare | you well;
K. Henry VIII, I, 3, 21: —

I'm glad | 'tis there: | now I | would pray | our mon|sieurs;
Ib., V, 2, 325: —

This is | the ape | of form, | mónsieur | the nice.

In this last line the word might indeed be read as an iambic, but it is a trochee after the pause. That *monsieur*, in Shakespeare's time, was generally accented on the first syllable, seems also to be confirmed by four of its six different spellings which occur in the first Folio, viz. *mounsieur, mounseur, mounsier,* and *monsier;* the fifth and sixth being *monsieur* (*passim*) and *monsieuer* (in As You Like It, I, 2, 173). The diphthong *ou* in the first syllable (which replaces the original *o*), recalls such words as *counsel* (*consilium*), *fountain* (*fontana*), *mountain* (*montana*), &c., and shows that the word was brought under the Teutonic accentuation. Also Dryden (Heroic Stanzas upon the Death of Oliver, &c. st. 23) accents it on the first syllable: —

Than the | light Món|sieur the | grave Don | outweighed,

and in 1663 we meet with the spelling *Mounser* which admits of no other accent but on the first syllable; see Rye, England as seen by Foreigners, p. 187. In more recent times, however, the French accentuation of the word has been re-instated and has kept its ground to the present day, just as it has been the case with the adjectives *divine, extreme, obscure,* &c. It should be added that all other passages in Shakespeare where *monsieur* occurs, are in prose.

CDXLIV.

Iach. They are in a trunk,
Attended by my men.

IB., I, 6, 197.

Qy. read: *Attended by my* MAN? Only in l. 53 of this very
scene Iachimo has spoken of his man and informed us that
he is strange and peevish.

CDXLV.

Sec. Lord. You cannot derogate, my lord.

IB., II, 1, 48.

There can be little doubt that these words belong to the
First and not to the Second Lord, and that Dr Johnson's
alteration of the prefix is right. Eight lines lower down the
common text should be replaced by the following arrangement: —

First [instead of *Sec.*] *Lord.* I'll attend your lordship.

[*Exeunt Cloten and First Lord.*

Sec. Lord. That such a crafty devil &c.

Compare note on I, 2, 40 seqq.

CDXLVI.

Ah, but some natural notes about her body,
Above ten thousand meaner moveables
Would testify, to enrich mine inventory.

IB., II, 2, 28 SEQQ.

Qy. read and point: —

Ah, but some natural notes about her body, —
Above ten thousand meaner moveables
They'ld testify, — t' enrich mine inventory?

6

CDXLVII.

The troasure of her honour. No more. To what end?

IB., II, 2, 42.

No Alexandrine, but a blankverse with an extra-syllable before the pause; scan:—

The treas|ure of | her hon|our. No more. |.T'what end?

Two lines *infra memory* is to be read as a dissyllable, which makes the line a regular blankverse. Mr Fleay declares l. 44 to be an Alexandrine, but makes no mention of l. 42.,

----

CDXLVIII.

Swift, swift, you dragons of the night, that dawning
May bare the raven's eye!

IB., II, 2, 48 SEQ.

In my conviction the last words should neither be understood literally, nor can we suppose, as Dyce justly remarks, that Shakespeare would turn night to a raven at the same moment when introducing her as a goddess. Shakespeare, who was conversant with so many facts of natural history, may possibly have been aware that the raven, to introduce Mr R. Gr. White's remark *ad loc.*, 'is the most matinal [*sic*, read *matutinal*] bird, even more so than the lark'. But I greatly doubt that his audience, unadulterated cockneys as they were, should have been so intimately acquainted with the ways and habits of the raven as to understand an allusion so far-fetched and altogether foreign to the context. To me Sir Thomas Hanmer seems to have hit the mark in attributing the raven's eye (or raven-eye) to dawning itself; Iachimo expresses the wish that dawning might soon bare or ope its eye which is as dark as the raven. Hanmer proposes to read: *its* raven eye, but no alteration is needed; least of all Collier's suggestion, BLEAR *the raven's eye*, which has been energetically rejected by Dyce as being 'most ridiculous'.

CDXLIX.

And winking Mary-buds begin
  To ope their golden eyes:
With every thing that pretty is,
  My lady sweet, arise:
    Arise, arise.

IB., II, 3, 25 SEQQ.

Read, of course, *that pretty* BIN, as printed by Hanmer; his alteration of *every thing*, however, is not needed, although *bin* is the third person plural; see Morris, Outlines of English Accidence, s. 295, p. 182; Mätzner's Engl. Grammatik (1ˢᵗ Ed., I, 367); Al. Schmidt, Shakespeare-Lexicon, s. *Be*. *Every* is not unfrequently used as a collective and as such governs the plural; compare, e. g., Much Ado about Nothing, III, 4, 60 seq.: Nothing I; but God send every one their heart's desire! Lucrece, 125: —

And every one to rest themselves betake.

Dryden, Annus Mirabilis, st. 15: —

It seems as every ship their sovereign knows,

where the singular *knows* is required by the rhyme.

It may be as well to add, that also *all* has sometimes the plural after it; compare, e. g., Byron's Childe Harold, III, 62: —

All that expands the spirit, yet appals,
Gather around these summits;

Ib., IV, 162: —

          Are exprest
All that ideal beauty ever bless'd.

6*

CDL.

The one is Caius Lucius.
   Cym.   A worthy fellow.

                       IB., II, 3, 60.

Mr Fleay scans this line : —
   Th' one's Ca|ius Lu|cius. | A wor|thy fel|low.
But the verse has evidently an extra-syllable before the pause
and is to be scanned : —
   The one | is Ca|ius Lu|cius. A wor|thy fel|low.

CDLI.

Yet you are curb'd from that enlargement by
The consequence o' the crown, and must not soil
The precious note of it with a base slave,
A hilding for a livery, a squire's cloth,
A pantler, not so eminent.

                 IB., II, 3, 125 SEQQ.

The only critic that has queried this passage, is Collier.
'We may, he says rather hesitatingly, also suspect a misprint
in the word "note".' — *Note* is surely a misprint; read *robe*.
What the poet here calls the '*precious* ROBE *of the crown*' in
K. Henry V, IV, 1, 279 is styled : —
   The intertissued robe of gold and pearl,
and is there enumerated among the king's attributes. What
reader of Shakespeare does not also recall Cleopatra's
words : —
   Give me my robe, put on my crown; I have
   Immortal longings?
'You must not soil, says Cloten, the regal robe with a base
slave, a hilding born to wear a livery, or a squire's cloth at
best.' The context sufficiently shows that this is what the

poet had in his mind and wanted to express, and I need
not dwell on the circumstance that, throughout our play,
garments play a conspicuous part in Cloten's thoughts and
even influence his actions. — The misprint *foyle* for *foyle* in
the Ff would not be worth mentioning, but for the fact that
Dr Al. Schmidt, who in his Shakespeare-Lexicon has proved
a stickler for the correctness of the first Folio, upholds the
lection *foil.*

CDLII.

I am sprited with a fool,
Frighted, and anger'd worse.

IB., II, 3, 144 SEQ.

The meaning which has been missed in the late Professor
Hertzberg's translation, is: I am not only sprited by a fool,
but what is still worse, frighted and angered by the loss of
my bracelet; the anonymous conjecture on l. 141:—

How now! [*missing the bracelet*]. Pisanio!

having indeed hit the mark.

CDLIII.

But the worst of me. So, I leave you, sir.

IB., II, 3, 159.

A syllable pause line; scan:—

But th' worst | of me. | ᴗ So, | I leave | you, sir.

The same scansion occurs in the first hemistich of the next
line (*To th' worst | of dis|content*).

---

86 CYMBELINE.

CDLIV.

In these fear'd hopes,
I barely gratify your love.

Ib., II, 4, 6 seq.

This is the reading of all the Ff; according to Collier (2nd Ed.) *ad loc.* the words mean 'in these hopes which I fear may never be realised' [!]. Dyce has adopted Tyrwhitt's conjecture *sear'd*, as he (most justly) 'cannot think that the original reading here is to be defended on the supposition that "fear'd hopes" may mean "fearing hopes" or "hopes mingled with fears".' The Rev. H. Hudson reads *'sere hopes'*; *'sere hopes*, he explains, are withered hopes; as they would naturally be in their Winter's state.' The hopes of Posthumus, however, are neither *feared* (by whom?), nor *seared* or *withered*, but they are DEAR *hopes*, and this, in my humble opinion, is what the poet wrote.

CDLV.

Let it be granted you have seen all this, — and praise.

Ib., II, 4, 92.

Mr Fleay wrongly reckons this line among the Alexandrines. Read and scan: —

Let it | be grant'd | you've seen | all this, | — and praise.
Compare Abbott, s. 472.

CDLVI.

Iach.   Then, if you can,
                          [*Showing the bracelet.*
Be pale: I beg but leave to air this jewel; see!
And now 'tis up again.

Ib., II, 4, 95 seqq.

'In II, 4, 96, says Mr Fleay, arrange "be pale" iu l. 95'. —
This, of course, would only be transferring the Alexandrine
from l. 96 to l. 95. To me it seems to admit of little
doubt, that *See* forms a most energetic interjectional line.
Arrange: —

Then, if you can,

Be pale: I beg but leave to air this jewel;
See!   [*Showing the bracelet.*
And now 'tis up again.

CDLVII.

Must be half-workers? We are all bastards.

IB., II, 5, 2.

The conjectures of Pope, Capell (S. Walker, Crit. Exam., III,
322), and Keightley are needless. The verse is a syllable
pause line; scan: —

Must be | half-work|ers? ⌐ | We are | all bast|ards.

CDLVIII.

For wearing our own noses. That opportunity.

IB., III, 1, 14.

This line, left unnoticed by Mr Fleay, has both an extra-
syllable before the pause and a trisyllabic feminine ending.

CDLIX.

Cym. You must know,
Till the injurious Romans did extort &c.

IB., III, 1, 47 SEQQ.

I have no doubt that this speech does not belong to Cymbeline, but to the Queen who has been interrupted rather

uncourteously by her son and whom the king expressly wishes to end, especially as by her action she undoubtedly indicates her desire of saying something more. My suspicion is confirmed by the following remarkable metrical fact. Dr Abbott, s. 514, has ingeniously shown that 'interruptions are sometimes not allowed to interfere with the completeness of the speaker's verse.' Now the first line of the speech in question exactly completes the last line of the Queen's antecedent speech (l. 33), although an interruption by no less than three speeches, two from Cloten and one from the king, has taken place. This is the line: —

And Britons strut with courage. — You must know.

The words *We do* in l. 54 are assigned to '*Cloten*' by Collier and Dyce, to '*Cloten and Lords*' by the Cambridge Editors. Either prefix may be right, yet I own that this once I think it safer to side with Collier and Dyce than with the Cambridge Editors; the Lords, in my opinion, expressing their assent merely by gestures.

CDLX.

Though Rome be therefore angry: Mulmutius made our laws.

IB., III, 1, 59.

One of Mr Fleay's Alexandrines. I have no hesitation in accepting Steevens's emendation, i. e., in discarding the words '*made our laws*' which are evidently either a marginal gloss intended to explain or to replace '*Ordained our laws*', or a dittography. The verse is a syllable pause line: —

Though Rome | be there|fore an|gry: ⊥ | Mulmu|tius.

CDLXI.

Thyself domestic officers — thine enemy.

IB., III, 1, 65.

According to Mr Fleay an Alexandrine with 'the cesura after the eighth syllable'. I take it to be a blankverse with a trisyllabic feminine ending (*enemy*). Three lines farther on Mr Fleay would make his readers believe in another Alexandrine with the cesura after the ninth syllable (!). In my conviction it is a blankverse with an extra-syllable before the pause; *defied* is to be pronounced as a monosyllable; see note CCLXXIX. Scan: —

For fu|ry not | to be | resist|ed. Thus d'fied.

CDLXII.

Pis. How! of adultery? Wherefore write you not
What monster's her accuser? Leonatus!

IB., III, 2, 1 SEQ.

Adultery is to be pronounced as a trisyllable. The Ff have an interrogation after *accuse* (*accuser* is Capell's correction) and a colon after *Leonatus*, which latter has been replaced by an exclamation in all, or almost all, modern editions, a dash being moreover introduced before *Leonatus*. Point: —

Wherefore write you not
What monster's her accuser, Leonatus?

CDLXIII.

O, not like me;
For mine's beyond' beyond — say, and speak thick.

IB., III, 2, 57 SEQ.

The meaning is, My longing is beyond being beyond yours.
Compare Macbeth, I, 4, 21 : —
More is thy due than more than all can pay.

CDLXIV.

And our return, to excuse: but first, how get hence.

Ib., III, 2, 66.

The Rev. H. Hudson reads on his own responsibility: *how
to get hence*. 'As *hence*, he says in his Critical Note *ad loc.*,
is emphatic here, *to* seems fairly required; and *get* is evidently
in the same construction with *excuse*. To be sure, the insertion of *to* makes the verse an Alexandrine; but the omission
does not make it a pentameter [Mr Hudson clearly means
to say a *blankverse*]. The omission was doubtless accidental.'
— I do not see, why the line without Mr Hudson's addition,
should not be taken for a blankverse; scan : —
And our | return, | t'excuse: | but first, | how get | hence.
A closely analogous ending occurs in l. 17 of the following
scene : —
But be|ing so | allow'd: | to ap|prehend | thus.

CDLXV.

Prithee, speak,
How many score of miles may we well ride
'Twixt hour and hour?

Ib., III, 2, 70.

'Twixt hour and hour, according to the Rev. H. Hudson,
means: 'Between the same hour of morning and evening;
or between six and six, as between sunrise and sunset, in
the next speech.' — But Imogen's longing that is 'beyond

beyond' and wishes for a horse with wings, would not have
been satisfied with such a slow rate of travelling; what she
wishes to know is, how many score of miles she may ride
from the stroke of one hour to that of the next, and Pisanio
makes the disheartening reply, only one score from one rising
of the sun to the next. Compare III, 4, 44: To weep 'twixt
clock and clock.

CDLXVI.

That run i' the clock's behalf. But this is foolery.

IB., III, 2, 75.

Not an Alexandrine as Mr Fleay would have it, but a blankverse with a trisyllabic feminine ending (*foolery*). Line 77
which has not been noticed by Mr Fleay, has likewise a trisyllabic feminine ending and the words *to her* are to be run
into one another: —

She'll home | t' her fa|ther: and | provide | me pres|ently.

Possibly, however, *She'll* had better be added to the preceding line: —

Go bid | my wom|an feign | a sick|ness: say, | she'll
Home to | her fa|ther: and | provide | me pres|ently.

CDLXVII.

To see me first, as I have now. Pisanio! man!
Where is Posthumus?

IB., III, 4, 3 SEQ.

Arrange with S. Walker, Crit. Exam., III, 323, and Mr Fleay: —

To see me first, as I *crave* now. Pisanio!
Man! Where's Posthumus?

Crave, proposed by the Cambridge Editors (?), is no doubt
the true reading.

CDLXVIII.

Some jay of Italy
Whose mother was her painting, hath betray'd him.
IB., III, 4, 51 SEQ.

'The figure, says Mr R. Gr. White *ad loc.*, here approaches
extravagance,' and in the Globe Edition the passage is marked
with an obelus.   Nevertheless the true blue conservatives in
Shakespearian criticism uphold the old text against those
wild conjecturing folks that are not willing to kiss the first
Folio; they even reckon such strained figures among the
beauties of the poet's diction.   In support of their inter-
pretation they refer the reader to IV, 2, 81 seqq., where
Cloten's tailor is termed his 'grandfather': —

          he made those clothes
Which, as it seems, make thee.

There is, however, this difference between the two passages
that the tailor, mentioned in the latter, is a real human
being, whereas the painting is not.   It is true that, if the
tailor is to be considered as Cloten's grandfather, Cloten's
dress must be taken to be his father; but the poet does not
startle us by such a grotesque figure — it is merely implied.
Besides it is a common proverbial saying that 'Fine feathers
make fine birds', whilst nobody ever heard it said, that 'Fine
painting makes a fine harlot.'   Still less can the phrase be
countenanced by the well-known passage in K. Lear, II, 2, 60:
'a tailor made thee'.   A similar thought occurs strangely enough
in A. V, sc. 4, l. 123 seq. of our play: —

Sleep, thou hast been a grandsire, and begot
A father to me;

but this is indeed the natural father of Posthumus.   The Rev.
R. Roberts (in N. and Q., Sept. 29, 1883, p. 241 seq.) has
discovered two passages manifestly bearing upon the present

line; the one occurs in Shelton's Translation of Don Quixote (2^d Ed., 1652, lib. I, pt. 4, chap. 24, p. 133), the other in a pamphlet entitled: 'Newes from the New Exchange; or, The Commonwealth of Ladies. London, printed in the Yeere of Women without Grace, 1650.' From the former passage it would appear that somebody 'said that his arm was his father, his works his lineage'; nothing certain, however, can be said of it, since Mr Roberts has not favoured his readers with the context. The second passage is to the following effect: 'If Madam Newport should be linkt with these Ladies, the chain would never hold; for she is sister to the famous Mistress Porter . . . . . and to the more famous Lady Marlborough (whose Paint is her Pander).' I am greatly surprised to find that neither Mr Roberts, nor Dr Brinsley Nicholson who has reproduced the above extracts in The New Shakspere Society's Transactions 1880—2, p. 202, should have thought of the possibility that here we may have got the clue to the line under discussion and that Shakespeare probably wrote:—

Some jay of Italy
Whose *pander* was her painting, hath betray'd him.

————

CDLXIX.

And thou, Posthumus, that didst set up.

Ib., III, 4, 90.

In order to regulate the metre Capell has repeated *thou* after *Posthumus*, and all editors after him have followed in his wake. I have no doubt that Capell's division of the lines is right, but there is no need of an insertion, as the verse clearly belongs to the much-discussed class of syllable pause lines; scan:—

And thou, | Posthu|mus, ⌐ | that didst | set up.

————

CDLXX.

Pis. I'll wake mine eye-balls blind first.

Ib., III, 4, 104.

The lection of the Ff: *I'll wake mine eye-balls first* cannot
possibly be right, and most editors have therefore adopted
Hanmer's addition *blind* after *eye-balls.* Staunton defends
the old reading on the strength of a passage in Lust's
Dominion (I, 2; Dodsley, ed. Hazlitt, XIV, 104): —

> I'll still wake,
> And waste these balls of sight by tossing them
> In busy observations upon thee.

Dyce, however, cannot think (and very properly too) that
wake, in this passage, should govern *eye-balls;* he conceives
the meaning to be, 'I'll still keep myself awake, and waste
these balls,' &c. He is, therefore, convinced that in the line
under discussion some such word as *blind* seems to be required
after *eye-balls* in order to complete both sense and metre.
To me the very passage from Lust's Dominion seems to point
in a very different direction, in as much as it suggests the
conjectural emendation: —

> I'll *waste* mine eye-balls first.

Compared to this almost imperceptible alteration the insertion of *blind* is no doubt needlessly bold. As to the metre,
the verse is to be numbered with the syllable pause lines;
scan : —

> I'll *waste* | mine eye-|balls first. | ⌣ Where|fore then.

A confusion between *waste* and *wake* seems also to have
taken place in Timon of Athens, II, 2, 171: I have retired me
to a wasteful cock, instead of which unintelligible twaddle
Mr Swynfen Jervis has most ingeniously proposed to read:
I have retired me to a WAKEFUL COÜCH.

CDLXXI.

Nor no more ado
With that harsh, noble, simple nothing,
That Cloten, whose love-suit hath been to me
As fearful as a siege.

IB., III, 4, 134 SEQQ.

Dr Brinsley Nicholson proposes to read, *ignoble noble* (N. and Q., Sept. 29, 1883, p. 241). This conjecture spoils the metre, although *ignoble* seems to be the word wanted instead of *noble*, but not conjointly with•it. Perhaps we should read: —

With that | harsh, *that* | *igno|ble*, sim|ple noth|ing,
That Cloten, &c.

All other conjectures to which this line has given rise, from Rowe to Collier's so-called MS-Corrector downwards, may be passed over with silence. Compare S. Walker, Crit. Exam., I, 33.

CDLXXII.

Pis.   If not at court,
Then not in Britain must you bide.
    Imo.   Where then?
Hath Britain all the sun that shines? Day, night,
Are they not but in Britain? I'the world's volume
Our Britain seems as of it, but not in't;
In a great pool a swan's nest: prithee, think
There's livers out of Britain.
    Pis.   I am most glad
You think of other place.

IB., III, 4, 137 SEQQ.

The words *Where then?* have been continued to Pisanio by Hanmer, but Pisanio has 'consider'd of a course' and has

made up his mind; he has no occasion to ask '*Where then?*'
Imogen, on the contrary, has just put the question to Pisanio: —
What shall I do the while? where bide? how live?
She now asks again: *Where then?*, but she cannot possibly
be the speaker of the two following lines. The original
distribution of the lines, in my opinion, was this: —

> *Pis.*   If not at court,
> Then not in Britain must you bide.
> *Imo.*   Where then?
> *Pis.* Hath Britain all the sun that shines? Day, night,
> Are they not but in Britain?
> *Imo.*   I'the world's volume
> Our Britain seems as of it, but not in't;
> In a great pool a swan's nest: prithee, think
> There's livers out of Britain.
> *Pis.*   I am most glad
> You think of other place.

It may be left to the reader to form his own opinion of
Capell's conjecture, *What then?* and of Mr P. A. Daniel's
transposition of *of it* and *in it*.

———

CDLXXIII.

> Now, if you could wear a mind
> Dark as your fortune is, &c.

IB., III, 4, 146 SEQ.

In my opinion Warburton's conjecture *mien* for *mind* should
be installed in the text without reserve, so much the more
as it would appear that *mien* was frequently spelt and pronounced *mine* and could therefore easily be mistaken for
mind; compare Dryden, ed. W. D. Christie (Clarendon Press,
1874) p. 228. — Al. Schmidt, Shakespeare-Lexicon, s. *Mien*,
thinks differently.

———

CDLXXIV.

Beginning nor supplyment.

Imo. Thou art all the comfort.

IB., III, 4, 182.

Mr Fleay wrongly classes this line with the Alexandrines; scan:—

Begin|ning nor | supply|ment. Thou'rt all | the com|fort.

CDLXXV.

A prince's courage. Away, I prithee.

IB., III, 4, 187.

Either a four foot line with an extra syllable before the pause:—

A prin|ce's cour|age. Away, | I pri|thee,

or a syllable pause line:—

A prin|ce's cour|age. ⊥ | Away, | I pri|thee.

CDLXXVI.

Appear unkinglike.

Luc. So, sir: I desire of you.

IB., III, 5, 7.

Scan:—

Appear | unking|like.

Luc. So, sir: | I d'sire | of you.

See note CCLXXIX. I think it merely owing to an oversight that this line has not been brought forward as an Alexandrine by Mr Fleay. Compare S. Walker, Crit. Exam., III, 325.

7

CDLXXVII.

Madam, all joy befall your graçe.
  Queen.   And you!

IB., III, 5, 9.

The Ff continue the words *And you!* to Lucius. To me the
conjectural emendation introduced into the text of the Globe
Edition by the Cambridge Editors seems indeed palmarian.
Lucius bids farewell to the King, the Queen, and Cloten
successively and it seems obvious that all three should reply,
especially the Queen who appears to be fond of speaking
not only in her own name, but even in that of others. The
words *And you* cannot, therefore, belong to any other
character but to her; least of all can they be addressed to
Cloten by the Roman ambassador, as only in l. 12 the latter
turns to Cloten and takes his leave from him by a cordial
shaking of the hand.

CDLXXVIII.

She looks us like
A thing more made of malice than of duty.

IB., III, 5, 32 SEQ.

Here too the Cambridge Editors (for I hope I shall not be
wrong in fathering this anonymous emendation upon them)
have hit the mark in suggesting *on's* for *as* in FA, or *us* in
FBCD: —

She looks *on's* like
A thing more made of malice than of duty.

CDLXXIX.

That will be given to the loudest noise we make.

IB., III, 5, 44.

FA: *th' lowd of noise.* I think Rowe's conjecture *the loudest noise* preferable to that of Capell, *the loud'st of noise*, as, in accordance with Rowe and Singer, I feel convinced that *of* is a misprint for *'st* or *st.* Singer wrongly prints *th' loud'st noise*, instead of *th' loudest noise.*

———

CDLXXX.

Prove false!
    Queen.   Son, I say, follow the king.

IB., III, 5, 53.

Rowe's division of the lines is right, the conjectures suggested by Steevens, Jackson, S. Walker, &c., however, are needless.
Scan: —

Prove false! |
    Queen.   ⌣ Son, | I say, | follow | the king.

———

CDLXXXI.

Pisanio, thou that standst so for Posthumus!
He hath a drug of mine; &c.

IB., III, 5, 56 SEQ.

The transition in these lines from the second to the third person, abrupt and awkward though it be, yet seems to have proceeded from the poet's own pen, especially as the same irregularity has already occurred before (III, 3, 104): —

        they took thee for their mother,
And every day do honour to her grave.

A third instance of a cognate kind (a transition from the third to the second person) occurs in A. IV, sc. 2, l. 217 seq.: —

With female fairies will his tomb be haunted,
And worms will not come to thee.

7*

'Alack, no remedy!', (III, 4, 163) is the only remark to be
made: on these and similar deviations from correct and
grammatical diction, by which not only 'Cymbeline', but
Shakespeare's latest plays in general, are marked. See Dyce's
note on I, 1, 118 (While sense can keep it on).

———

CDLXXXII.

Clo. I love and hate her: for she's fair and royal,
And that she has all courtly parts more exquisite
Than lady, ladies, woman; from every one
  The best she hath, and she, of all compounded,
Outsells them all.

                                        IB., III, 5, 70 SEQQ.

Line 71, left unnoticed by Mr Fleay, has a trisyllabic feminine ending (*exquisite*). In the next line, this dreadful *crux*,
I suspect, though not without diffidence, that we should
read: —
          Than lady, *lass,* or woman; &c.
except it should be deemed admissible to introduce into the
text of Shakespeare the diminutive *lassie*, in which case the
reading *Than lady,* LASSIE, *woman* would come nearest to the
old text. I am well aware that *lass* (or *lassie*) is chiefly a
pastoral word, its use, however, is not restricted exclusively
to that homely kind of poetry, as it is proved by a signal
instance in Shakespeare. In Antony and Cleopatra, V, 2,
318 seq. Charmian, speaking of the dead Queen of Egypt,
says: —
          Now boast thee, death, in thy possession lies
          A lass unparallel'd.
Cleopatra is certainly anything but pastoral, and Imogen
deserves the praise of being '*a lass unparallel'd*' in a far

higher and nobler sense than she. In our passage the poet
evidently alludes to the different classes of womankind, of
every one of which Imogen has the best. She possesses the
nobleness and dignified manners of a lady, the innocence
and sprightliness of a young girl, and the true womanly
feeling of a matron, and thus, of all compounded, outsells
them all. The strained explanation of the old text given by
Singer cannot find favour in the eyes of scholars trained to
the strict exegetical rules of classical philology. According
to him Shakespeare means to say that Imogen has the courtly
parts more exquisite 'than any lady, than all ladies, than
all womankind.' The passage from All's Well that Ends
Well (II, 3, 202: to any count; to all counts; to what is man)
quoted by Singer, is not to the point, in so far as it is
intelligible and correct, two distinguishing qualities of which
the passage in Cymbeline cannot boast.

———

CDLXXXIII.

Close villain,
I'll have this secret from thy heart; or rip
Thy heart to find it.

IB., III, 5, 85 SEQQ.

Arrange and read with Dyce's second edition:—

. Close villain, I
Will have this secret from thy heart, &c.

———

CDLXXXIV.

Pis. [*Aside*] I'll write to my lord she's dead. O Imogen.

IB., III, 5, 104.

S. Walker, Crit. Exam., III, 326, needlessly proposes to
omit *to*; scan: —

'I'll write | to m'lord | she's dead.' | O Im|ogen.

Compare note CCCVI (Vol. II, p. 176).

CDLXXXV.

Be but duteous, and true preferment shall tender itself to thee.

IB., III, 5, 159 SEQ.

S. Walker, Crit. Exam., III, 326, very properly asks: 'What
has *"true* preferment" to do here?' and proposes to point:
'be but duteous and true, preferment' &c. *True* certainly
cannot be joined to *preferment*, but must necessarily refer to
Pisanio, as Cloten in l. 110 has required *true service* from
Pisanio and repeats his admonition immediately after (l. 162:
Come, and be true) to which admonition Pisanio in his soliloquy replies: —

true to thee

Were to prove false, which I will never be,
To him that is most true.

On the other hand, the omission of *and* before *preferment*
seems harsh; perhaps a slight transposition may help us to
the true reading, viz. *be but duteous-true, and preferment* &c.
Compare S. Walker, Crit. Exam., I, 21 seqq. Merchant of Venice,
III, 4, 46 (*honest-true*); Cymbeline, V, 5, 86 (*duteous-diligent*).

CDLXXXVI.

Pis. Thou bid'st me to my loss: for true to thee
Were to prove false, which I will never be,
To him that is most true.

IB., III, 5, 163 SEQQ.

Collier's MS-Corrector: *to* THY *loss*, which lection has been introduced into the text by the Rev. H. Hudson who thinks *my loss* 'little better than unmeaning here.' Quite the contrary. To Cloten's exhortation 'be but duteous-true, and preferment shall tender itself to thee', Pisanio replies: 'no, the way thou bidst me go, would not lead to my preferment, but to my loss, in so far as it would make me false to my master who is the truest of all.'

CDLXXXVII.

Imo. To Milford-Haven.

Bel. What's your name? IB., III, 6, 59 SEQ.

These two short lines should be joined into one, which is to be scanned and read:—

Imo. To Mil|ford Ha|ven. ⌣ |

Bel. What *is* | your name?

The reading *What is* was proposed by Capell. — Two lines further on we have no choice left but to adopt Hanmer's correction *embarks* instead of *embark'd*, so much the more as in A. IV, sc. 2, l. 291 seq. we learn from Imogen that she has by no means given up her journey to Milford-Haven and consequently is still in hopes of joining Lucius there. By the way it may be remarked, that Hanmer's edition (Oxford, 1770) does not read *embarques*, as reported in the Cambridge Edition, but *embarks*.

CDLXXXVIII.

I should woo hard but be your groom. In honesty.

IB., III, 6, 70.

This line, not noticed by Mr Fleay, is not an Alexandrine, but has a trisyllabic feminine ending (*honesty*).

CDLXXXIX.

Cowards father cowards and base things sire base.

IB., IV, 2, 26.

S. Walker, Versification, 145 and Crit. Exam., I, 153 dis-
syllabizes *sire*. There is, however, room for two other scansions, viz.: —

Cow'rds fa|ther cow|ards and | base things | sire base;
Cowards | fath'r cow|ards and | base things | sire base.

———

CDXC.

Know'st me not by my clothes?
   Gui.   No, nor thy tailor, rascal.

IB., IV, 2, 81.

One of Mr Fleay's Alexandrines. Pope omitted *rascal*, no
doubt on purely metrical grounds. There is, however, another
argument which speaks in favour of this omission, and this
is the marked contrast between the two characters of Cloten
and Guiderius. Cloten, from the very moment of his entrance,
heaps the most abusive language on his adversary, whereas
Guiderius studiously refrains from retaliating. Guiderius says
(l. 78 seq.): —

Thy words, I grant, are bigger, for I wear not
My dagger in my mouth.

Only twice he retorts: in l. 72 seqq. (A thing more slavish &c.,
which is moderate language enough) and in l. 89 (thou double
villain). I am, therefore, inclined to agree with Pope, not
only because *rascal* spoils the metre, but at the same time because it contradicts the well-defined character of Guiderius.
It is no doubt an actor's addition.

———

CDXCI.

Yield, rustic mountaineer.   [*Exeunt, fighting.*
    Re-enter BELARIUS *and* ARVIRAGUS.
Bel. No companies abroad?

IB., IV, 2, 100 SEQ.

Metrically considered this is a very curious line, as it admits of no less than three different scansions. First the two hemistichs may be considered as two short lines, and as such they are printed by Dyce, in the Cambridge and Globe Editions, &c. Or they may be connected so as to form an Alexandrine, which has been done by Mr Fleay, and here it must be owned that such Alexandrines (or trimeter couplets) are by no means of rare occurrence. The third way of scanning the line is to read *mountainer* and pronounce the word as a trisyllabic feminine ending before the pause. We shall then have to deal with a regular blankverse, and I need scarcely add that in my conviction this is the true scansion. The Ff certainly read *mountaineer*, but in l. 71 of our scene they exhibit the spelling *mountainers* which S. Walker, Versification, 224, is mistaken in declaring an erratum, as according to his own showing it occurs also in Chapman's The Widow's Tears, IV, 1. Besides it corresponds exactly with the spellings *pioner* and *enginer* in Hamlet I, 5, 163 and III, 4, 207; compare my second edition of Hamlet, p. 114 (note on *Climatures*).

CDXCII.

And burst of speaking, were as his: I am absolute.

IB., IV, 2, 106.

A Spenserian Alexandrine according to Mr Fleay; I think it a blankverse with a trisyllabic feminine ending (*absolute*).

CDXCIII.

Bel. Being scarce made up,
I mean, to man, he had not apprehension
Of roaring terrors; for defect of judgement
Is oft the cause of fear. But, see, thy brother.

IB., IV, 2, 109 SEQQ.

Theobald's conjectural emendation *th' effect* instead of *defect*
has been admitted into the text of the Globe Edition; the
other attempts at correcting this evidently corrupted passage
are hardly worth mentioning. Perhaps we should read and
arrange:—

for defect of judgment
Is oft the cause of *fearlessness.* But see!
Thy brother!

I cannot attach any great weight to the objection which will
probably be raised against this conjectural emendation, that
fearlessness does not belong to Shakespeare's vocabulary, as
fearless, fearful, and *fearfulness* do; besides the word comes
nearer to the *ductus literarum* of the old copies than if *courage*
or *valour* should be suggested instead. At all events I feel
sure that this is the thought that was in the poet's mind.

———

CDXCIV.

So the revenge alone pursued me! Polydore.

IB., IV, 2, 157.

No Alexandrine, but a blankverse with a trisyllabic feminine
ending (*Polydore*). Mr Fleay does not mention this line. /.

CDXCV.

For, his return.

Bel.   My ingenious instrument.

                                 Ib., IV, 2, 186.

Either ; —

   For his | return. |

     Bel.,   My inge|nious in|strument,

or a syllable pause line with a trisyllabic feminine ending: —

  For his | return. |

     Bel.   ∪ My | inge|nious in|strument.

———

CDXCVI.

Is Cadwal mad?

    Bel.   Look, here he comes.

                               Ib., IV, 2, 195.

A defective line thus completed by S. Walker, Crit. Exam., II, 145: —

   Is Cadwal, mad?

     Bel.   Cadwal! — Look, here he comes!

However ingenious this conjecture may be, yet I cannot refrain from giving it a somewhat different turn by assigning the exclamation *Cadwal!* to Guiderius: —

   Is: Cadwal mad? Cadwal!

    Bel: Look, here, he comes.

———

CDXCVII.

Gui. Cadwal, I cannot sing: I'll weep and word it with thee.

                            Ib., IV, 2, 240.

An Alexandrine, if we are to believe Mr Fleay; but *Cadwal* palpably forms an interjectional line and is printed as such by Dyce, in the Cambridge and Globe Editions, &c.

———

CDXCVIII.

Gui. Nay, Cadwal, we must lay his head to the east;
My father has a reason for it.'

IB., IV, 2, 255 SEQ.

'What was Belarius' "reason", says Mr R. Gr. White *ad loc.*, for
this disposition of the body in the ground I have been unable
to discover.' — Belarius' reason is no doubt to be found in
the custom which prevailed in the Christian church to bury
the dead with their heads looking to the East, where the
Saviour had lived and from whence he is believed to
re-appear on the day of the last judgment. For the same
reason the early Christians turned their face to the East
when praying and the churches face the same part of the
horizon, in so far as the chancel which contains the altar,
the consecrated wafers, the crucifix, &c. generally occupies
the eastern end of the building. See J. Kreuser, *Der christ-
liche Kirchenbau* (Bonn, 1851) I, 42 seqq. Id., *Wiederum christ-
licher Kirchenbau* (Brixen, 1868) I, 338 seqq. and II, 416 seqq.
Even the temples of classical antiquity are shown to have
been constructed according to the same plan by Heinrich
Nissen (*Das Templum.* Berlin, 1869). Our passage proves
that Shakespeare was conversant with some one or other of
these facts, though nobody can tell exactly with which; most
probably with the mode of making the dead in their graves
look to the East. Compare also Dr Johnson's note on
Hamlet, V, 1, 4: make her grave straight; Dr Johnson is
however wrong in so far as *straight* in this passage means
immediately.

CDXCIX.

But, soft! no bedfellow! — O gods and goddesses.

IB., IV, 2, 295.

Not noticed by Mr Fleay, although this verse might be pronounced to be an Alexandrine just as well as the rest. I
need scarcely say that I declare in favour of a blankverse
versus Alexandrine. Two different scansions would seem to
be admissible, viz.: —

But, soft! | no bed|fellow! O gods | and god|desses,

or: —

But, soft! | no bed|fellow! | O gods | and god|desses.

In the former case *bedfellow*, in the latter (which I cannot
but think preferable) *goddesses* is to be read as a trisyllabic
feminine ending.

_____

D.

For so I thought I was a cave-keeper.

IB., IV, 2, 298.

Rightly corrected by Collier's so called MS-Corrector: —

For *lo!* I thought I was a cave-keeper.

_____

DI.

Struck the main-top! O Posthumus! alas.

IB., IV, 2, 320.

The transposition proposed by Capell (according to the Cambridge Edition): *Posthumus, O! alas* seems needless. Scan
either: —

Struck the | maintop! | ⌣ O, | Posthum's! | alas,

or: —

Struck | the main|top! O, | Posthum's! | alas.

_____

DII.

> Which he said was precious
> And cordial to me, have I not found it
> Murderous to the senses? That confirms it home.
>
> IB., IV, 2, 326 SEQQ.

Scan : —

> Which he said was precious
> And cor|dial to | me, ⊥ | have I | not found | it
> Murd'rous | to th' sen|ses? That | confirms | it home.

It seems surprising that the last line has not been mentioned by Mr Fleay in his list of Alexandrines.

DIII.

> *Cap.* To them the legions garrison'd in Gallia
> After your will, have cross'd the sea.
>
> IB., IV, 2, 333 SEQ.

In my eyes the anonymous conjecture (by the Cambridge Editors?), according to which *To them* does not form part of the text, but of the stage-direction (*and a sooth-sayer to them*) is both above doubt and above praise. Compare amongst other passages the stage-direction in Coriolanus I, 4: *To them a Messenger.*

DIV.

> Attending
> You here at Milford-Haven with your ships.
>
> IB., IV, 2, 334 SEQ.

FACD: *with your ships*; FB: *with you ships* (not *your*, as Dyce erroneously says). Neither of these two lections can be right. Qy. *with* YON *ships*? It may safely be assumed that Milford-Haven with its ships is to be seen from the spot where Lucius is conversing with the officers, as we have heard from Imogen (III, 6, 5) that Pisanio showed it to her before parting with her. Or is recourse to be had to the correction *with* THEIR *ships*?

———

DV.

And gentlemen of Italy, most willing spirits.

IB., IV, 2, 338.

This line which Mr Fleay takes to be an Alexandrine, in my opinion has a trisyllabic feminine ending before the pause; scan: —

And gen|tlemen |'of It|aly, most wil|ling spir|its.

———

DVI.

Cap. With the next benefit o' the wind.

Luc.   This forwardness.

Scan : —   IB., IV, 2, 342.

Cap. With the | next ben|'fit of | the wind. |

Luc.   This for|wardness.

Forwardness is to be read as a trisyllabic feminine ending. The line might have figured among Mr Fleay's Alexandrines.

———

DVII.

They 'll pardon it. — Say you, sir?

Luc.   Thy name?

Imo.   Fidele, sir.

IB., IV, 2, 379.

I subscribe unhesitatingly to Hanmer's correction of the line, viz. the contraction of *pardon it* and the omission of the second *sir*; scan : —

They 'll par|don't. Say | you, sir? |

Luc.   Thy name? |

Imo.   Fide|le.

———

DVIII.

My friends,
The boy hath taught us manly duties: let us
Find out the prettiest daisied plot we can,
And make him with our pikes and partisans
A grave.

IB., IV, 2, 396 SEQQ.

S. Walker, Crit. Exam., III, 327, proposes to omit *thee* after
father in the preceding line (l. 395) and to arrange the passage as in the Ff. I should prefer to join *My friends* with
l. 397; to contract *let us* and transfer it to the following
line; and to omit *out* in l. 398: —

My friends, the boy hath taught us manly duties:
Let's find the prettiest daisied plot we can,
And make him with our pikes and partisans
A grave.

DIX.

The hope of comfort. But for thee, fellow.

IB., IV, 3, 9.

Capell: *But for thee*, THEE, *fellow*; compare S. Walker, Crit.
Exam., II, 146. Dr Abbott, s. 453, scans: —

The hope | of com|fort. But | for thee, | féllow.

Thus the line is made to end in a trochee, since, according
to Dr Abbott, 'the old pronunciation "fellów" is probably not
Shakespearian.' The verse is undoubtedly a syllable pause
line: —

The hope | of com|fort. $\perp$ | But for | thee, fel|low.

DX.

Pis. Sir, my life is yours;
I humbly set it at your will; but, for my mistress,
I nothing know where she remains,. why gone,
Nor when she purposes return. Beseech your highness,
Hold me your loyal servant.
First Lord. Good my liege,
The day that she was missing &c.

IB., IV, 3, 12 SEQQ.

Arrange:—

Pis. Sir, my life is yours;
I humbly set it at your will; but for
My mistress, I nothing know where she remains,
Why gone, nor when she purposes return.
Beseech your highness, hold me your loyal servant.
First Lord. Good my liege,
The day that she was missing &c.

Thus we get rid of the two apparent Alexandrines in lines
13 and 15. Lines 14 and 16 have extra-syllables before the
pause (*mistress* and *highness*).

———

DXI.

All parts of his subjection loyally. For Cloten.

IB., IV, 3, 19.

The words *For Cloten* have been placed in a separate line
by Capell. According to Mr Fleay the line is an Alexandrine with the cesura after the tenth (!) syllable. I have no
doubt that *loyally* is to be read as a trisyllabic feminine
ending before the pause: —

All parts | of his | subject;ion loy|ally. For Clo|ten.

Troublesome in line 21, and *jealousy* in l. 22 are trisyllabic
feminine endings too.

———

8

DXII.

We grieve at chances here. Away!

Ib., IV, 3, 35.

Hanmer completes this line by adding: *Come let's* before *Away!*, which involves an unpleasant repetition of *Let's withdraw* in l. 32. S. Walker, Versification, 273, would arrange:—

We grieve at chances here.

Away.

This seems even more unlikely than Hanmer's addition. I do not see the necessity of filling up the line; if, however, such a completion should be deemed indispensable, I should suggest to read:—

We grieve at chances here. Away, *my lords.*

———

DXIII.

Wherein I am false I am honest; not true, to be true.

Ib., IV, 3, 42.

A Spenserian Alexandrine, if we are to believe Mr Fleay. I suspect that we ought to scan:—

Wherein | I'm false | I'm hon|est; not true | t' be true.

———

DXIV.

Revengingly enfeebles me; or could this carl.

Ib., V, 2, 4.

An Alexandrine according to Mr Fleay. The line, I think, has a trisyllabic feminine ending before the pause; scan:—

Reveng|ingly | enfee|bles me; or could | this carl.

———

DXV.

Post. Still going? [*Exit Lord.*] This is a lord! O noble
misery.

IB., V, 3, 64.

Not noticed by Mr Fleay. Pope, Theobald, and Hanmer
omit *Still going?*, whilst S. Walker (Crit. Exam., III, 327),
Dyce, and the Rev. H. Hudson place these words in a separate line. In my humble opinion both parties are wrong.
Instead of *this is* read *this'* (see Abbott, p. 343) and pronounce *misery* as a trisyllabic feminine ending: —

Still go|ing? This' | a lord! | O no|ble mis|ery.

DXVI.

And so I am awake. Poor wretches that depend.

IB., V, 4, 127.

One of Mr Fleay's Alexandrines. I strongly suspect: —
And so | I'm 'wake. | Poor wretch|es that | depend.
Compare Abbott, s. 460.

DXVII.

Tongue and brain not; either both or nothing.

IB., V, 4, 147.

Tongue is to be read as a monosyllabic foot; the conjectures
proposed by Rowe, Pope, Johnson, Steevens, and others may
therefore be stowed away in the critical lumber-room. Scan: —
Tongue | and brain | not; eith|er both | or noth|ing.

DXVIII.

O'ercome you with her show, and in time.

IB., V, 5, 54.

8 *

Here too all conjectures are needless; scan: —

O'ercome | you with | her show, | ◡ and | in time.
A similar scansion holds good with respect to l. 62, where
Hanmer inserted *Yet* before *Mine eyes*; scan: —

We did, | so please | your high|ness. ⌐ | Mine eyes.
Both verses are syllable pause lines.

DXIX.

Cym. All that belongs to this.
Iach.   That paragon, thy daughter.

IB., V, 5, 147.

Another of Mr Fleay's Alexandrines. The line has a trisyllabic feminine ending before the second pause. Scan: —

Cym. All that | belongs | to this. |
Iach.   That par|agon, thy daugh|ter.

DXX.

For feature, laming
The shrine of Venus, or straight-pight Minerva,
Postures beyond brief nature.

IB., V, 5, 163 SEQQ.

'By a sharp torture' something like a meaning may be
'enforced' from these lines, *shrine*, in the opinion of the
editors, being used here and elsewhere in the sense of *statue*.
The only critics, as far as I know, that take exception against
this awkward metonymy in the present passage and declare
the line to be corrupt, are Bailey (who absurdly suggests
SHRINKING *Venus*) and the late Prof. Hertzberg in the notes
on his translation of our play; but his attempts at healing
the corruption are inferior to his arguments and unsatisfactory

even in his own eyes. I imagine that Shakespeare wrote *swim* instead of *shrine*, thus contrasting the swimming gait of Venus with the stiff and strait-built stature of Minerva, a contrast well known to every student of ancient art. It must be admitted that the substantive *swim* does not belong to Shakespeare's vocabulary; it is used, however, by B. Jonson, Cynthia's Revels, II, 1: Save only you wanted the swim in the turn, and: Both the swim and the trip are properly mine. Compare notes LXVII and LXVII*.

DXXI.

O, get thee from my sight.

IB., V, 5, 236.

A mutilated line to which the name of *Pisanio* is to be added: —

O, get | thee from | my sight, | Pisa|nio.

See note on I, 1, 41.

DXXII.

Breathe not where princes are.

Cym.   The tune of Imogen.

IB., V, 5, 238.

Declared to be an Alexandrine by Mr Fleay. *Imogen*, however, is clearly a trisyllabic feminine ending; compare *ante* l. 227, where the second *Imogen* is to be pronounced as a dissyllable: —

Imo|gen, Im|'gen! Peace, | my lord; | hear, hear.

Compare also note on Antony and Cleopatra, IV, 9, 23 seqq., where the first *Antony* is likewise a trisyllable, the second a dissyllable.

DXXIII.

Think that you are upon a rock; and now
Throw me again.

IB., V, 5, 262 SEQ.

Mr R. Gr. White has hit the mark in suggesting the emendation, *Think she's upon your neck*, only he should have con-
formed it to the metre; read: —

Think *that she is* upon your neck; and now
Throw me again.

———

DXXIV.

With unchaste purpose and with oath to violate.

IB., V, 5, 284.

Not mentioned by Mr Fleay; *violate* is a trisyllabic feminine
ending. Compare Childe Harold, IV, 8: —

The invi|'late is|land of,| the sage | and free,

and Tennyson, Idylls of the King (London, 1859) p. 160: —

Not vi|'lating | the bond | of like | to like.

———

DXXV.

Arv.   In that he spake too far.
Cym. And thou shalt die for 't.
Bel.   We will die all three:
But I will prove that two on's are as good
As I have given out him.

IB., V, 5, 309 SEQQ.

Arrange: —

Arv.   In that he spake too far.
Cym. [*To Bel.*] And thou shalt die for it.
Arv.   We will die all three.
Bel. But I will prove that two on's are as good
As I have given out him.

Cymbeline's speech (*And thou* &c.) is shown by the context to be addressed to Belarius, and not to Arviragus, who has committed no offence whatever. The two persons condemned to death by the King are Guiderius and Belarius, whilst Arviragus is allowed to live; consequently he is the only person to whom the words, 'We will die all three' can be assigned.

DXXVI.

Gui. And our good his.
Bel.   Have at it then, by leave.
Thou hadst, great king, a subject who
Was call'd Belarius.

IB., V, 5, 314 SEQQ.

All endeavours of healing this manifestly corrupt passage have proved insufficient. I refrain, therefore, from reproducing them and merely beg to offer a contribution of my own. I suspect that we should read and arrange: —

Gui. And our good *is your good.*
Bel.   Have at it then.
By leave! Thou hadst, great king, a subject who
Was call'd Belarius.

Of this I feel certain that the words *By leave!* are not addressed to Guiderius and Arviragus, but to the king, and so Capell and Dyce seem to have understood the passage. For greater perspicuity's sake the stage-direction: [*To Cym.*] might be added at the beginning of l. 315.

DXXVII.

Your pleasure was my mere offence, my punishment.

IB., V, 5, 334.

Not noticed by Mr Fleay; *punishment* is a trisyllabic feminine
ending. — The same scansion occurs in l. 344 (also left unnoticed by Mr Fleay) where *loyalty* is a trisyllabic feminine
ending.

DXXVIII.

Unto my end of stealing them. But, gracious sir.

Iв., V, 5, 347.

Pope omits *gracious* and Mr Fleay takes the line to be an
Alexandrine with the cesura after the eighth syllable. I have
no doubt that the verse, like so many others, has a trisyllabic feminine ending before the pause; scan: —

Unto | my end | of steal|ing 'em. But, gra|cious sir.

DXXIX.

The thankings of a king.
      Post.   · I am, sir.

Iв., V, 5, 407.

A syllable pause line; scan: —

The thank|ings of | a king. |
      Post.   ᴗ I | am, sir.

There is no need whatever of conjecturing or correcting.*)

---

*). As at p. 65 seq. I have reproduced the introductory words
of my Letter to C. M. Ingleby, Esq., I must here make room for the
concluding words too. They were these: 'This, my dear Ingleby, is
my critical mite on "Cymbeline". I am perfectly aware that the
revision and explanation of this play will still be a match for ages
to come and wish above all that the state of your health may shortly
allow you to do your part and complete your edition. Not even
the stanchest defender of the Folio can go so far as to deny that by

DXXX.

Bring in our daughter, clothed like a bride,
For the embracements even of Jove himself.

PERICLES I, 1, 6 SEQ.

Line 6 admits of a twofold scansion: —

Bring in | our daugh|ter, cloth|èd like | a bride,

or, which I think preferable: —

Bring in | our daugh|ter, ⌣ | clothed like | a bride.

In the following line the conjecture *Fit for* (by the Cambridge Editors?) should unhesitatingly be installed in the text and the article *the*, inserted by Malone, but omitted by the anonymous critics, as unhesitatingly be retained: —

Fit for *the* embracements even of Jove himself.

———

DXXXI.

Per. See where she comes, apparell'd like the spring,
Graces her subjects, and her thoughts the king
Of every virtue gives renown to men!

IB., I, 1, 12 SEQQ.

———

the continued efforts of editors and critics the text of Shakespeare has been brought a great deal nearer to its original purity than when it was printed by Isaac Jaggard and Ed. Blount in 1632. Shakespeare's versification too is far better understood by the commentators of to-day than by Nicholas Rowe and the rest of the eighteenth-century-editors. ".Step by step the ladder is ascended." These facts justify the hope that the twentieth century may enjoy a still more correct text of the immortal dramatist and possess a deeper insight into his language and metre than we can boast of. May we then be remembered as having assisted in handing down the torch from one generation to the other. *Vale faveque.* Always believe me, dear Ingleby, Yours very sincerely K. E. Halle, On the Ides of March, 1885.'

Qy. read: —

Grace is her *subject*, and her *thought's* the king?
Thought's is a happy conjecture by the Cambridge Editors (?).
It should not be overlooked that throughout this passage the
poet makes use of the singular: *Her face the book* (l. 15);
Sorrow (l. 17); *testy wrath* (ib.); *Her face* (l. 30); *Her count-
less glory* (l. 31). This circumstance serves no doubt to
corroborate the conjectures of the Cambridge Editors and
myself.

DXXXII.

Good sooth, I care not for you.

Ib., I, 1, 86.

Add the stage-direction: [*Pushes the Princess back*]. Compare A. V, sc. 1, l. 127: when I did push thee back. The
stage-direction: *Takes hold of the hand of the Princess*, added
by Malone after l. 76, in my opinion misses or rather contradicts the intention of the poet as expressed in the text.

DXXXIII.

Ant. He hath found the meaning, for which we mean
To have his head.
He must not live to trumpet forth my infamy,
Nor tell the world Antiochus doth sin
In such a loathed manner.

Ib., I, 1, 143 SEQQ.

Arrange and read: —

Ant. He hath found the meaning,
For which we mean to have his head; he must
Not live to trumpet forth my infamy,
Nor tell the world Antiochus doth sin
In such a loathed manner *with his daughter*.

He hath is to be contracted into a monosyllable; see note on Antony and Cleopatra, III, 13, 82 seq. *For which* is the reading of all the old editions; Malone, in consequence of his wrong division of the lines, added the article before *which*, an addition which, although very well compatible with my arrangement, yet seems needless.

DXXXIV.

Because we bid it. Say, is it done?
    Thal.   My lord,
'Tis done.
    Ant. Enough.
                         IB., I, 1, 158 SEQQ.

The division of the old copies is quite correct and should not have been altered by Steevens whose arrangement has even been adopted by the Cambridge (and Globe) Editors. Scan: —

Because | we bid | it. ⏕ | Say, is | it done?
    Thal. My lord, 'tis done.
    Ant. Enough.

DXXXV.

I'll make him sure enough: so farewell to your highness.
                         IB., I, 1, 169.

Sure enough is a trisyllabic feminine ending before the pause: —

I'll make | him sure | enough; so fare|well to | your high|ness.

See note on Antony and Cleopatra, I, 4, 7 seq.

DXXXVI.

And danger, which I fear'd, is at Antioch.

IB., I, 2, 7.

S. Walker, Versification, 100, suggests, *fear'd, 's at Antioch*, which on account of the pause after *fear'd*, does not seem likely. I think we should omit *at* before *Antioch* and read:—

The danger, which I fear'd, is Antioch.

The comma at the end of the preceding line should be altered to a colon, if not a full stop.

DXXXVII.

And then return to us. [*Exeunt Lords.*] Helicanus, thou
Hast moved us: what seest thou in our looks?

IB., I, 2, 50 SEQ.

Helicanus is to be pronounced as a trisyllabic word (= *Hel'-canus*); compare *Pericles* which is several times used as a dissyllable (see note on II, 1, 132) and *Leonine* which in A. IV, sc. 1, l. 30 and A. IV, sc. 3, l. 9 has likewise the quality of a dissyllable, whereas in A. IV, sc. 3, l. 30 it is a trisyllable. See note on Antony and Cleopatra, I, 2, 134 (*Enobarbus*). — Line 51 is a syllable pause line; scan: —

Hast moved | us: ⏊ | what seest | thou in | our looks?

DXXXVIII.

Per. Thou know'st I have power
To take thy life from thee.
Hel. [*Kneeling*] I have ground the axe myself;
Do you but strike the blow.
Per. Rise, prithee, rise.
Sit down: thou art no flatterer:

I thank thee for it: and heaven forbid ▸

That kings should let their ears hear their faults chid.

IB., I, 2, 57 SEQQ.

Arrange, read, and scan: —

    Per.   Thou know'st *I've* power

To take thy life from thee.

    Hel. [*Kneeling*]   *I've* ground the axe

Myself; do you but strike the blow, *my lord.*

    Per. Rise, prithee, rise. Sit down: thou art no flatterer;

I thank | thee for | it; ⌣ | and heaven | forbid

That kings should let their ears hear their faults chid.

In all old and modern editions, as far as I know, *myself*
belongs to l. 58; for the transfer of this word to the next
line, I must answer as well as for the addition of *my lord.*
Flatterer, in l. 60, is a trisyllabic feminine ending. L. 61 is
a syllable pause line and does not stand in need of Steevens's
conjecture HIGH *heaven.* With respect to l. 62 I entirely
agree with Dyce.

DXXXIX.

Hel. Well, my lord, since you have given me leave to speak.

IB., I, 2, 101.

Pronounce *m'lord.* Compare *supra* note on The Winter's
Tale I, 2, 161 (Vol. II, p. 176) and note on Cymbeline III,
5, 104.

DXL.

Freely will I speak. Antiochus you fear,

And justly too, I think, you fear the tyrant,

Who either by public war or private treason

Will take away your life.

IB., I, 2, 102 SEQQ.

A perfect muddle. Read and scan: —

   Freely | will I | speak. -/- | You fear | the ty|rant
   Antiochus, and justly too, I think,
   Who either by public war or private treason
   Will take away your life.

Line 102 is a syllable pause line. That *either* is frequently contracted into a monosyllable, need hardly be mentioned; compare S. Walker, Versification, 103.

DXLI.

Or till the Destinies do cut his thread of life.

In., I, 2, 108.

This line is by no means an Alexandrine, but has a trisyllabic feminine ending before the pause; scan: —

   Or till | the Dest|'nies do cut | his thread | of life.

DXLII.

But should he wrong my liberties in my absence.

In., I, 2, 112.

Can the meaning be: What, if he should encroach on my princely rights in my absence? Or is *my liberties* to be regarded as a corruption? Collier assures his readers that 'we may be reasonably sure that "my liberties" ought to be "*thy* liberties."' This, however, is anything but an improvement. By the context I am led to imagine that Shakespeare wrote TYRE'S *liberties*; *liberties* to be pronounced as a disyllable. In the reply which Helicanus makes to this speech, a line seems to have been lost, the purport of which apparently was: *In order to prevent such a misfortune* we shall mingle our bloods together &c.

DXLIII.

And so in ours: some neighbouring nation.

Ib., I, 4, 65.

Qy.: *and so* IS *ours?*

DXLIV.

Lord. That's the least fear; for, by the semblance.

Ib., I, 4, 71.

How are we to scan: —

That's the | least fear; | for by | the semb|(e)lance,

or: —

That *is* | the least | fear; ⌣ | for by | the semb|lance?

DXLV.

And to fulfil his prince' desire.

Ib., II, GOWER, 21.

The majority of the old editions exhibit the reading *princes
desire* which has been altered by Rowe to *prince's Desire.*
Malone and all editors after him read *prince' desire.* To me
Rowe's correction seems no less admissible than Malone's.
For the monosyllabic pronunciation of *desire* compare *supra*
note CCLXXIX and note on Antony and Cleopatra, 1, 2, 126.

DXLVI.

Thanks, fortune, yet, that, after all my crosses,
Thou givest me somewhat to repair myself.

Ib., II, 1, 127 SEQ.

Should not Pericles have begun as well as ended his speech
with a rhyming couplet? May not Shakespeare have written: —

Thanks, fortune, yet, that after all *thy* [not *my*] crosses,
Thou givest me somewhat to repair *my losses?*

THY *crosses* is the reading of Delius, derived from Wilkins's novel; Malone, *my*; Qq and Ff, *all crosses*. *Heritage*, in the following line, is a trisyllabic feminine ending.

DXLVII.

Keep it, my Pericles; it hath been a shield. ·

IB., II, 1, 132.

Scan either:

Keep it, | my Per|icles; | it hath been | a shield, ·

or : —

Keep it, | my Per|'cles; it | hath been | a shield.

For the contraction of *it hath* compare note on Antony and Cleopatra, III, 13, 82 seq. *Pericles*, as a dissyllable, occurs in A. II, sc. 3, l. 81 : —

A gent|leman | of Tyre; | ᴗ my | name, Per|'cles;

in A. II, sc. 3, l. 87 (according to my arrangement; see note *ad loc.*); A. III, Gower, l. 60 (a four-feet line with an extra syllable before the pause); A. IV, sc. 3, l. 13, a line which seems to admit of a twofold scansion, viz.: —

When no|ble Per|'cles shall | demand | his child,

or : —

When no|ble Per|icles | shall d'mand | his child;

and A. IV, sc. 3, l. 23 : —

And o|pen this | to Per|'cles. I | do shame.

Compare note on I, 2, 50.

DXLVIII.

Sim. Opinion's but a fool, that makes us scan
The outward habit by the inward man.

IB., II, 2, 56 SEQ.

To the various conjectures proposed in order to heal l. 57 (which is undoubtedly corrupt) the following transposition of the preposition *by* may be added:—

By th' out|ward hab|it *⌐* | the in|ward man.

———

DXLIX.

Per. You are right courteous knights.

Sim.   Sit, sir, sit.

IB., II, 3, 27.

A syllable pause line; scan:—

You are | right court|eous knights. | ◡ Sit, | sir, sit.

Steevens's repetition of the first *Sit*, adopted by Singer, is unnecessary.

———

DL.

All viands that I eat do seem unsavoury,
Wishing him my meat. Sure, he's a gallant gentleman.

IB., II, 3, 31, SEQ.

Unsavoury and *gentleman* are trisyllabic feminine endings.

———

DLI.

Sim. He's but a country gentleman.

IB., II, 3, 33.

The line may easily be completed by the addition of *daughter:*—

Sim. Daughter, he's but a country gentleman.

———

DLII.

Sim. And furthermore tell him, we desire to know of him.

IB., II, 3, 73.

9

The metre of this line, if rightly understood, is completely right and no correction whatever is wanted. After the analogy of *father*, *mother*, *either*, *whether*, &c. *further* in *furthermore* is to be pronounced as one syllable; scan therefore: —

> And furth'r|more tell | him, we d'sire | to know | of
>   him.

As to *d'sire* see note on Antony and Cleopatra, I, 2, 126.

———

DLIII.

   Thai. He thanks your grace; names himself Pericles,
  A gentleman of Tyre,
Who only by misfortune of the seas
Bereft of ships and men, cast on this shore.

IB., II, 3, 86 SEQQ.

Read and arrange: —

    Thai. He thanks your grace;
  Names himself Pericles, a gentleman of Tyre,
Who *newly*, by misfortune of the seas
Bereft of ships and men, *was* cast on *th'* shore.

For the pronunciation of *Pericles* compare the note on II, 1, 132. *Only*, the reading of all old and modern editions in l. 88, is decidedly wrong. *On this shore*, in l. 89, is the reading of the first Quarto and the Museum-copy of the second Quarto, whereas all the other old copies read *on* THE *shore*. Perhaps we had better read *on shore* or *ashore* (see The Tempest, II, 2, 128 — not 129, 121 [as printed in the Globe Edition] being a misprint for 120).

———

DLIV.

Even in your armours, as you are address'd,
Will very well become a soldier's dance.

IB., II, 3, 94 SEQ.

Qy. read *You'll* for *Will*?
You'll very well become a soldier's dance.

DLV.

Come, sir;
Here is a lady that wants breathing too:
And I have heard, you knights of Tyre
Are excellent in making ladies trip.

IB., II, 3, 100 SEQQ.

The words *Come, sir* have been placed in a separate interjectional line in the Globe Edition, which to me seems to be an unnecessary deviation from the old copies. I rather think that *sir* is misplaced and belonged originally to l. 102 which is thus promoted to the rank of a legitimate syllable pause line; —

Come, here's a lady that wants breathing too;
And I | have heard, | sir, ⌐ | you knights | of Tyre
Are excellent in making ladies trip.

All other conjectural emendations do not come half so near to the text of the old editions.

DLVI.

Hel. No, Escanes, know this of me.

IB., II, 4, 1.

This is the reading of the old copies. Malone: KNOW, *Escanes*; Steevens: *No*, NO, MY *Escanes*. Read: —
Now, Escanes, know this of me.

9*

DLVII.

Soon fall to ruin, — your noble self.

IB., II, 4, 37.

A syllable pause line; scan: —

Soon fall | to ru|in, ⌐ | your no|ble self.

Eight lines further on we meet with another syllable pause .
line of the same category: —

A twelve|month long|er, ⌐ | let me | entreat | you.

———

DLVIII.

Which yet from her by no means can I get.

IB., II, 5, 6.

The first and second Folios read, *Which from her* &c.; the
third and fourth, *Which* YET *from her* &c., an unnecessary
correction, that nevertheless has found admission into the
text of the Globe Edition, whilst the Cambridge Edition follows the two earlier Folios. In my humble opinion we have
to deal with a syllable pause line, however slight the pause
may appear: —

Which from | her ⌐ | by no | means can | I get.

Compare notes CCLIV, CCLXV, &c.

———

DLIX.

One twelve moons more she'll wear Diana's livery.

IB., II, 5, 10.

Livery is a trisyllabic feminine ending.

———

DLX.

Third Knight. Loath to bid farewell, we take our leaves.

IB., II, 5, 13.

Steevens: *Though loath*; Anon.: *Right loath*; Anon.: *will we.*
No expletive, however, is wanted, as the verse may safely be
reckoned among the syllable pause lines; scan: —

Loath to | bid fare|well, ⏌ | we take | our leaves.

In the same scene (l. 74) another syllable pause line occurs,
the pause of which is still slighter than that of l. 13: —

I am | glad on | it ⏌ | with all | my heart.

———

DLXI.

Will you, not having my consent.

IB., II, 5, 76.

If a blankverse should be thought requisite, the line may
easily be completed by the addition of *thereto*: —

Will you, not having my consent *thereto.*

———

DLXII.

As great in blood as I myself. —
Therefore hear you, mistress; either frame
Your will to mine, — and you, sir, hear you,
Either be ruled by me, or I will make you —
Man and wife.

IB., II, 5, 80 SEQQ.

No conjectural emendation of l. 81 is required. Arrange: —

As great in blood as I myself. Therefore
Hear you, mistress; either frame your will to mine, —
And you, sir, hear you, either be ruled by me, —
Or I will make you — man and wife.

———

DLXIII.

I nill relate, action may.

IB., III, GOWER, l. 55.

A syllable pause line; scan: —

I nill | relate, | ◡ act|ion may.

DLXIV.

Thy nimble, sulphurous flashes! O, how, Lychorida,
How does my queen? Thou stormest venomously.

IB., III, 1, 6 SEQ.

Line 6 has an extra syllable before the pause and a trisyllabic feminine ending. *Sulphurous* is to be pronounced as
a dissyllable. The trisyllabic pronunciation of *Lychorida* occurs
again in l. 65 of this very scene: —

Lying | with sim|ple shells. | ◡ O | Lychor|ida.

Venomously, in l. 7, is a trisyllabic feminine ending.

DLXV.

At careful nursing. Go thy ways, good mariner.

IB., III, 1, 81.

Mariner is a trisyllabic feminine ending.

DLXVI.

Death may usurp on nature many hours,
And yet the fire of life kindle again
The o'erpress'd spirits. I heard of an Egyptian
That had nine hours lien dead,
Who was by good appliance recovered.

  Re-enter a Servant, *with boxes, napkins, and fire.*
  Cer. Well said, well said; the fire and cloths.

IB., III, 2, 82 SEQQ.

This passage which in the Globe Edition is marked with an obelus before the words: *I heard of an Egyptian*, seems to admit of a remedy as satisfactory as it is easy. It strikes me that the lines: *I heard of an Egyptian ..... recovered*, do not belong to Cerimon, but should be assigned to either the First or Second Gentleman. Cèrimon's words, *Well said, well said*, are by no means addressed to the Servant and are not equivalent to *Well done*, as Collier, Delius, and the Rev. H. Hudson will have it, but form the reply to the Gentleman's appropriate and encouraging remark; their meaning is 'well or timely remarked'. That Shakespeare has given the thought a different turn from what it is in the novel can hardly be a matter of surprise or cause any difficulty to the critic. In order to restore the metre the words *Who was* should be transferred from the beginning of l. 86 to the end of l. 85, and in l. 86 Dyce's emendation (*appliances*) should be adopted:—

> That had | nine hou|(e)rs li|en dead, | who was
> By good appliances recoverèd.

I admit that the blankverse (l. 85) thus recovered, though metrically correct, yet has little to recommend it, but is rather lame and heavy. Critics of less strict observance may, perhaps, be better pleased by the insertion of the words *like this*, taken (with a slight variation) from the respective passage in Wilkins's novel. For the scansion of l. 86 (*recoverèd*) compare Titus Andronicus, V, 3, 120 (*deliverèd*). The passage, then, will read thus:—

> Death may usurp on nature many hours
> And yet the fire of life kindle again
> The o'erpress'd spirits.

First Gent.   I heard of an Egyptian
That had nine hours lien dead *like this*, who was
By good appliances recoverèd.
Re-enter a Servant, *with boxes, napkins, and fire.*
Cer. Well said, well said. [*To the Servant*] The fire
·   and cloths.

———

DLXVII.

The rough and woeful music that we have.

Ib., III, 2, 88.

Collier proposes *slow* for *rough*; most unlikely. Qy. either
soft, *low*, or *sweet?* Add the stage-direction: *Music behind
the scene.*

———

DLXVIII.

The viol once more: how thou stirr'st, thou block.

Ib., III, 2, 90.

Read *vial.* Dyce concludes from the context that Cerimon
means the musical instrument, not a small bottle. The more
I have been thinking of the passage, the more fully am I
convinced that the very contrary is true and that we must
side with R. Gr. White against Dyce. Cerimon is in a flutter
and speaks abruptly to the different bystanders; first he
approves of the well-timed remark of the First Gentleman;
then turns to the Servant; then orders the music to be
sounded; then impatiently calls for the vial; then incites the
music again. Let a trial be made on the stage, and I have
no doubt that the decision of the audience will be in favour
of *vial* against *viol*, although it may be admitted that the
latter does not absolutely contradict the context. *Stirrest*, in
the same line, is an evident corruption from *starest*. As
Cerimon repeatedly exhorts the servant to bestir himself, it

seems impossible that he should blame him for obeying his command. Besides, a block is not in the habit of stirring, but of staring. Mr Fleay, in the Transactions of the New Shakspere Society, 1874, p. 217, reads and scans:—

The vi|ol once | more; how | thou stirr'st, | thou block.

But had not the verse be better scanned as a syllable pause line:—

The *vial* | once more; | ∪ how | thou *starest*, | thou block?

DLXIX.

Into life's flower again!
First Gent.   The heavens.

IB., III, 2, 96.

A defective line to which Steevens proposed to add *sir*; the right addition, I think, is *my lord*. Two more defective lines follow at short intervals, viz. III, 2, 103 and III, 2, 110. In the former verse, where the arrangement of the old editions seems preferable to that of Malone, *again*, in the latter, *neighbours* would seem to have been the word that has dropt out. These, then, are the three lines when completed:—

Into life's flower again! The heavens, *my lord*;
To make | the world | twice rich. | ∪ Live | *again*;
For her relapse is mortal. Come, come, *neighbours*.

Dyce thinks it most probable that the last line should be completed by a third repetition of *Come*.

DLXX.

To have bless'd mine eyes with her!
Per.   We cannot but obey.

IB., III, 3, 9.

Mr Fleay declares this line to be an Alexandrine. I rather think that *eyes with her* is a trisyllabic feminine ending before the pause; scan : —

T' have blest | mine eyes | wi' her. We can|not but | obey. Compare IV, 1, 50 and see note on Antony and Cleopatra, I, 4, 7 seq.

_____

DLXXI.

Cle. We'll bring your grace e'en to the edge o' the shore,
Then give you up to the mask'd Neptune and
The gentlest winds of heaven.

IB., III, 3, 35 SEQQ.

Instead of the nonsensical *mask'd Neptune* Dyce proposes VAST *Neptune*; S. Walker (Crit. Exam., III, 336) MOIST *Neptune*. The context, I think, sufficiently shows that a wish for a happy voyage is implied and that we should read CALM or CALMEST *Neptune* : —

Cle. We'll bring your grace e'en to the edge o' th' shore,
Then give you up to the *calmest* Neptune and
The gentlest winds of heaven.

'*The calmest Neptune*' would strictly correspond with '*the gentlest winds*' which, if Cleon's prayer take effect, will this once waft the 'sea-tost' Pericles safely and smoothly back to Tyre.

_____

DLXXII.

Deliver'd, by the holy gods.

IB., III, 4, 7.

A mutilated line; add: *of a child* : —
Deliver'd *of a child*, by the holy gods.
Or should we be allowed to supply, *of child* : —
Deliver'd, by the holy gods, *of child* ?

_____

DLXXIII.

Where you may abide till your date expire.

IB., III, 4, 14.

A syllable pause line; scan: —

Where you | may 'bide | ∪ till | your date | expire.

Malone's conjecture is unnecessary.

DLXXIV.

Might stand peerless by this slaughter.

' IB., IV, GOWER, l. 40.

An unmetrical line, unless it be taken for a trochaic verse, or *Might* be allowed to stand for a monosyllabic foot. An acceptable correction might be derived from a similar passage in Antony and Cleopatra, I, 1, 40 (We stand up peerless), viz.: —

Might stand *up* peerless by this slaughter.

DLXXV.

Leon. I will do't; but yet she is a goodly creature.

Dion. The fitter, then, the gods should have her. Here she comes weeping for her only mistress' death. Thou art resolved?

Leon. I am resolved.

IB., IV, 1, 9 SEQQ.

Malone's conjectural emendation *I'll* for *I will*, in l. 9, admits of no doubt. He is also decidedly right in printing (1790) Dionyza's speech as verse and in ending the first line at *Here*. Add to these corrections Percy's ingenious emendation *old nurse's* instead of the nonsensical *only mistress'* and the original text will be restored: —

Leon. I'll do't; but yet she is a goodly creature.

Dion. The fitter, then, the gods should have her. Here She comes, weeping for her old nurse's death. Thou art resolved.

Leon.   I am resolved.

DLXXVI.

Mar. No, I will rob Tellus of her weed.

IB., IV, I, 14.

No is certainly wrong and both Steevens's and Malone's conjectures (*No, no* and *Now*) are anything but improvements. Qy. read and scan : —

So; | I will | rob Tel|lus of | her weed?

So is a monosyllabic foot; compare The Works of John Marston, ed. J. O. Halliwell (Lon., 1856) Vol. III, p. 135 : —

Tha[is]. So, | there's one | fool shipt | away. | Are your Cross-points discovered? Get your breakfast ready.

Marina, in uttering this exclamation of 'acquiescence or approbation', as Al. Schmidt, s. v. *So*, defines it, casts a contented glance at the flowers in her basket.

DLXXVII.

Lord, how your favour's changed With this unprofitable woe! Come, give me your flowers, ere the sea mar it. Walk with Leonine; the air is quick there, And it pierces and sharpens the stomach. Come, Leonine, take her by the arm, walk with her.

Mar. No, I pray you; I'll not bereave you of your servant.

Dion.   Come, come;
I love the king your father, and yourself,
With more than foreign heart.

IB., IV, 1, 25 SEQQ.

Come, in l. 27, should be transferred to l. 26, which by this transposition becomes a regular blankverse:—

     With this | unprof|ita|ble woe. | ◡ Come!

The way to the restoration of the rest of l. 27 has been shown by the Rev. H. Hudson who supplanted the stupid lection of the old copies, *ere the sea mar it*, by the most ingenious emendation: *on the sea-margent*, which may be brought still nearer to the original *ductus literarum* by being altered to, *there the sea-margent*. I am well aware that *on the sea-marge walk*, or *there the sea-marge walk*, would lend the line a smoother flow, but these readings would be two or three steps farther removed from the old text, so that no choice is left to a strict critic. Instead of *quick*, which is the uniform reading of all the old copies, the Cambridge Editors (?) have proposed to read *quicker*. *Pierces*, in l. 29, is to be pronounced as a monosyllable, like *belches* (III, 2, 55), *breathes* (III, 2, 94), and similar words; see Abbott, s. 471. In the same line *well* has been inserted by Steevens; I should willingly do without this expletive, if I felt sure that no objection would be raised to the completion of the line by the archaic form *sharpeneth*. Line 30 is a syllable pause line; scan:—

     Leonine, | take her | by th' arm; | ◡ walk | with her.

The pronunciation of *Leonine* has been discussed *supra*, note on I, 1, 50. Marina's reply has hitherto been printed either as prose or in two lines, both of which arrangements are certainly wrong and may be avoided by the omission of *I* before *pray*; the blankverse thus restored admits of two different scansions, either with an extrasyllable before the pause (*you*), or *bereave* to be pronounced as a monosyllable.

Being thus corrected, the passage will stand as follows: —

      Lord, how your favour's changed
With this unprofitable woe. Come!
Give me your flowers; *t*here the sea-mar*gent* walk
With Leonine; the air is quick there, and
It pierces and sharpens *well* the stomach. Come!
Leonine, take her by the arm; walk with her.
 Mar. No, pray you; I'll not bereave you of your servant.
 Dion. Come, come!
I love the king your father, &c.

———

DLXXVIII.

What! I must have a care of you.
 Mar.   My thanks, sweet madam.
             IB., IV, 1, 50.

Just like *eyes with her* in III, 3, 9 the words *care of you* are to be read as a trisyllabic feminine ending before the pause; scan: —

What! I | must have | a care | o' you.
 Mar.   My thanks, | sweet mad|am.
Compare note on Antony and Cleopatra, I, 4, 7.

———

DLXXIX.

That almost burst the deck.
 Leon. When was this?
            IB., IV, 1, 58 SEQ.

The words spoken by Leonine should be joined to the preceding line: —

That almost burst | the deck. |

Leon. ‿ When | was this?

DLXXX.

And yet we mourn: her monument.

IB., IV, 3, 42.

A defective line which should be completed by the insertion of *for her*: —

And yet we mourn *for. her*: 'her. monument.

It is a well-known fact that words immediately repeated or doubled (*her*: *her*) frequently mislead the copyist or compositor and are written or set up only once instead of twice.

DLXXXI.

Cle. Thou art like the harpy,

Which, to betray, dost, with thine angel's face,

Seize with thine eagle's talons.

IB., IV, 3, 46 SEQQ.

An evidently mutilated passage on which although several conjectures have been wasted already, yet I cannot refrain from increasing their number. The sense undoubtedly requires the addition of *allure*; read therefore: —

Thou art like the harpy,

Which, to betray, dost with thine angel's face

Allure, *and then* seize with thine eagle's talons.

Thus both the sentence and metre are completed. Compare V, 1, 45 seq.: —

She questionless with her sweet harmony

And other chosen attractions, would allure, &c.

DLXXXII.

Had I brought hither a corrupted mind,
Thy speech had alter'd it. Hold, here's gold for thee:
Persever in that clear way thou goest,
And the gods strengthen thee!
  Mar.   The good gods preserve you!
          IB., IV, 6, 111 SEQQ.

Arrange, scan, and read: —

Had I brought hither a corrupted mind,
Thy speech | had al|ter'd it. | Hold, here's | gold for | thee:
Persever in that clear way thou goest, and
The good gods strengthen thee!
  Mar.   The gods preserve you.

Although l. 112 is metrically correct, yet I should prefer to
read *alter'd it* as a trisyllabic feminine ending before the
pause and to scan: —

Thy speech | had al|ter'd it. Hold, here | *is* gold | for thee.

The transposition of *and* from l. 114 to l. 113, and of *good*
from Marina's speech to that of Lysimachus seems to be
imperatively demanded by the metre.

———

DLXXXIII.

Hear from me, it shall be thy good.
           IB., IV, 6, 123.

A syllable pause line; scan:—

Hear from | me, $\smile$ | it shall | be for | thy good.

———

DLXXXIV.

         Empty
Old receptacles, or common shores, of filth.
        IB., IV, 6, 185 SEQ.

I cannot imagine on what ground Malone's ingenious emendation *sewers* for *shores* can be denied admission into the text.

DLXXXV.

And in it is Lysimachus the governor.

IB., V, 1, 4.

Governor is a trisyllabic feminine-ending.

DLXXXVI.

Mar. If I should tell my history, it would seem
Like lies disdain'd in the reporting.
    Per.   Prithee, speak.

IB., V, 1, 119 SEQ.

Two different arrangements may be offered, both of which will remove the Alexandrine (l. 120). The first is to the following effect:—

If I | should tell | my his|tory, 't would seem | like lies
Disdain'd in the reporting.
    Per.   Prithee speak.

History is to be read as a trisyllabic feminine ending before the pause. The second arrangement begins at l. 118:—

You make more rich to owe?
    Mar.   If I should tell
My history, 't would seem like lies disdain'd
In the reporting.
    Per.   Prithee, speak.

History to be read as a trisyllable. It seems hard to tell which of these two arrangements possesses the better claim to be considered the poet's own.

DLXXXVII.

Mar. My name's Marina.
Per.   O, I am mock'd.

Ib., V, 1, 143.

Steevens needlessly inserted *sir*. It is a syllable pause line;
scan : —

My name's | Mari|na. ⌣̄ | O, I | am mock'd.

Another syllable pause line of the same kind occurs five
lines *infra* : —

To call | thyself | Mari|na. ⌣̄ | The name.

In the Globe Edition this latter passage (l. 148) is printed
as two short lines, whereas the two speeches at the head of
this note are printed as one line.

DLXXXVIII.

Per.   O, I am mock'd,
And thou by some incensed god sent hither
To make the world to laugh at me.
Mar.   Patience, good sir,
Or here I'll cease.
Per.   Nay, I'll be patient.

Ib., V, 1, 143 SEQQ.

Scan : —

To make | the world | to laugh | at me.
Mar.   Patience, | good sir,
Or here | I'll cease. |
Per.   Nay, I'll | be pa|ti-ent.

Laugh at me is to be read as a trisyllabic feminine ending.
Critics who do not think this scansion satisfactory, will be

obliged to arrange differently and to transpose in order to remove the Alexandrine: —

To make the world to laugh at me.
Mar.   *Good sir,*
Patience, or here I'll cease.
Per.   Nay, I'll be patient.

———

DLXXXIX.

You have been noble towards her.
Lys.   Sir, lend me your arm.
Per. Come, my Marina.
                    IB., V, 1, 264 SEQ.

Line 264 is an apparent Alexandrine which may be reduced to regular metre in a twofold manner. First by the omission of *Sir*: —

You have | been no|ble tow|ards her. Lend me | your arm.

Towards her may either be read as a trisyllabic feminine ending, or *her* be considered as an extra syllable before the pause, as *towards* is frequently pronounced as a monosyllable; see S. Walker, Versification, 119 seqq.; Al. Schmidt, Shakespere-Lexicon, s. *Toward.* The second way of restoring the passage lies in a different arrangement, viz.: —

You have | been no|ble tow|ards her. |
    Lys.   Sir, lend | me
Your arm. |
        Per.   Come, my | Mari|na.

Towards, in this case, to be pronounced as a dissyllable.

———

10*

DXC.

Who, frighted from my country, did wed.

IB., V, 3, 3.

The metrical difficulty of this line may be solved in a three-fold way. The first is to insert *once* before *did;* secondly, *country* may be pronounced 'as though an extra vowel were introduced between the *r* and the preceding consonant' (Abbott, s. 477); and lastly, the verse may be read as a syllable pause line: —

Who, fright|ed from | my coun|try, ⌣́ | did wed.

The reader may choose for himself.

DXCI.

She at Tarsus
Was nursed with Cleon; who at fourteen years
He sought to murder: but her better stars
Brought her to Mytilene.

IB., V, 3, 7 SEQQ.

For *who* in l. 8, which is the reading of all the old copies, Malone substituted *whom.* Qy. read: —

who at fourteen years
Her sought to murder: &c.?

DXCII.

A birth, and death?

Per. The voice of dead Thaisa!

Thai. That Thaisa am I, supposed dead And drown'd.

Per. Immortal Dian!

Thai. Now I know you better.

IB., V, 3, 34 SEQQ.

Arrange: —

A birth, and death?

Per. The voice of dead Thaisa!

Thai.   That Thaisa

Am I, supposèd dead and drown'd.

Per. Immortal Dian!

Thai.   Now I know you better.

Thaisa is regularly used by the poet as a word of three syllables with the accent on the penult; compare II, 3, 57; V, 1, 213; V, 3, 27; V, 3, 34; V, 3, 46; V, 3, 55; and V, 3, 70. Apart from the line under discussion (according to the received text) two passages would seem to contradict this rule, viz. V, 1, 212: —

To say my mother's name was Thaisa,

and V, 3, 4: —

At Pentapolis the fair Thaisa.

Both passages, however, are manifestly corrupted. The former has been ingeniously restored by the Cambridge Editors (?): —

To say my mother's name? It was Thaisa,

whilst the correction of the second is due to Malone: —

The fair Thaisa at Pentapolis.

Thus all three seeming exceptions are cleared away.*)

---

*) These notes on 'Pericles' (DXXX—DXCII) were first published in Prof. Kölbing's *Englische Studien*, Vol. IX, p. 278—290.

ADDENDA AND CORRIGENDA.

LVII.*

Collier, H. E. Dr. P. (1ˢᵗ Ed.), III, 315 seq., quotes some passages which go far to prove that '"statue" and "picture"
were sometimes used synonymously by old writers, as if the
custom of painting statues had confused their notions of the
difference between a statue and a picture.'

———

LXV.*

Compare Hamlet, III, 3, 74: and so he goes to heaven; ib., III,
3, 95: as hell, whereto it goes; The Merry Wives of Windsor,
II, 1, 52: If I would but go to hell for an eternal moment,
or so. — Another instance of *Gone to heaven*, occurs in Sherwood Bonner's Dialect Tales (New York, 1883) p. 182:
'Whar's your copper, Jack?' 'Gone to heaven, said Jack,
rolling his eyes.' It may be left to the reader's own judgment to decide whether or not the phrase is to be taken for
a euphemism in Jack's mouth as well as in that of Launcelot
Gobbo.

———

LXXV.*

Compare Faerie Queene, Bk. I, Canto 3, st. 23: —
Whom overtaking, they gan loudly *bray*.

———

LXXXV.*

Compare Cymbeline III, 6, 54 seq.: —
All gold and silver rather turn to dirt!
As 'tis no better reckon'd, but of those
Who worship dirty gods.
Pope, Essay on Man, IV, 279: —
Is yellow dirt the passion of thy life?

———

LXXXVI.*

Compare 2 Henry VI, IV, 2, 37 seqq.: —

Cade. For our enemies shall fall before us, inspired with the spirit of putting down kings and princes, — Command silence.

Dick. Silence!

LXXXVIII.*

Compare Westward Ho!, V, 1 (Webster, ed. Dyce, 1857, in 1 vol., p. 238 b): Sure, sure, I'm struck with some wicked planet, for it hit my very heart.

XCIII.*

Compare Dekker and Webster, Westward Ho!, I, 1 (Webster, ed. Dyce, 1857, in 1 vol., p. 210 a): *Bird*[*lime*]. My good lord and master hath sent you a velvet gown here: do you like the colour? threepile, a pretty fantastical trimming! . . . . . *Mist. Just*[*iniano*]. What's the forepart? *Bird.* A very pretty stuff. — lb., V, 3 (Webster, ed. Dyce, p. 240 b): How many of my name, of the Glowworms, have paid for your furred gowns, thou woman's broker? — These passages, I think, speak eloquently in favour of the supposition that 'a suit of sables' means a garment trimmed with sable.

XCVI.*

Compare Pericles, II, 3, 6: —

Since every worth in show commends itself.

XCIX.*

Compare Westward Ho!, II, 3 (Webster, ed. Dyce, 1857, in
1 vol., p. 222 b): Come, drink up Rhine, Thames, and Mean-
der dry. (An exhortation to drinking Rhenish wine at the
Steelyard.)

CII.*

I am extremely sorry to say that on p. 4 seq. I have committed one of the most glaring dittographies, the conjectural
emendation *bounty'd* having been printed already in the first
volume of these Notes, p. 5, note X.

CXIX.*

Compare for similar violent *enjambements* B. Jonson, Catiline,
III, 8 (Folio; Works, Lon., Moxon, 1838, in 1 vol., III, 3,
p. 288 a): —

    The flax and sulphur are already laid
    In, at Cethegus' house; so are the weapons.

Volpone, V, 2 (Folio; Works &c., V, 1, p. 199 b): —

    Shew them a will: open that chest, and reach
    Forth one of those that has the blanks; I'll straight
    Put in thy name.

CXXIII.*

Compare notes CCLXXI and CCCV. Lord Byron, Sardana-
palus, II, 1 (Poetical Works, in 1 vol., Lon., 1864, p. 254 b): —

    May I | retire? |
    Arb.   Stay.
    Bel.   Hush! | let him go | his way.

Mark Antony Lower, The Song of Solomon [in] the Dialect
of Sussex, &c. London, 1860, p. IV: —
Set'n down, and let'n stan;
Come agin, and fet'n anon.

___

CXXXIV.*

At p. 23, l. 11 read: —
Therefore let's once again join hands in friendship.

___

CXCV.*

Compare the following passage from Westward Ho!, V, 4
(Webster, ed. Dyce, 1857, in 1 vol., p. 243 b): —
Ten[*terhook*]. Marry, you make bulls [qy. *gulls?*] of
your husbands.
Mist. Ten[*terhook*]. Buzzards, do we not? out, you
yellow infirmities! do all flowers show in your eyes like
columbines?

___

CCLIV.*

Line 7. Instead of· *dissyllabication* read *dissyllabification*.

___

CCLXXIX.*

P. 143, l. 9 seq. read: Richard II, IV, 1, 148 (*r'sist*);
Richard III, III, 5, 109 (*r'course*); ib., V, 3, 186 (*r'venge*).
In the line taken from Richard II the first *it* (after *Prevent*)
may be read as an extra-syllable before the pause: —
Prevent | it, resist | it, let | it not | be so.
Compare Marlowe, Edward II, I, 1, 29 (Marlowe's Works, ed.
Dyce, in 1 vol., p. 183 b): —
And, as | I like | your d'scours|ing, I'll | have you.

Or should we read: —

And, as | I like | your d'scours|ing, *I* | *will* have | you?
Mr Fleay, in his edition of Edward II, accents *discoursing*,
without, however, producing an authority for such an accentuation. It may be added that in the American Dialect
Tales by Sherwood Bonner (New York, 1883) we frequently
meet with similar abbreviations such as *b'lieve*, *b'long*, *p'r'aps*,
'bey (= obey), *'salt* (= assault; p. 35), *'Onymus* (= Hiero-
nymus; p. 68 seqq.), *s'ppose*, &c.

CCLXXX.*

The same rhythm (*Long* in the accented part of the measure)
is also to be found in Cymbeline, III, 7, 10: —

His absolute commission.   Long live Cæsar,

and in Marlowe's Edward II (Marlowe, ed. Dyce, 1870, in
1 vol., p. 204 b): —

Her[*ald*].   Long | live Ed|ward, Eng|land's law|ful lord.

In my eyes a strong accent on *Long* is essential in this kind
of exclamation and cannot be missed.

CCXCI.*

The same round sum of three thousand ducats occurs also
in Twelfth Night, I, 3, 22, where we are told by Sir Toby
Belch that Sir Andrew Aguecheek 'has three thousand
ducats a year'.

CCXCIII.*

At p. 161, last line but one, read 2 K. Henry IV (V, 4).

CCC.*

In Dekker and Webster's Comedy of Westward Ho! *sirrah* is frequently applied to married women, especially by their lady-friends. Compare Dyce's note on Westward Ho!, I, 2 (Webster, ed. Dyce, Lon., 1857, in 1 vol., p. 214a).

CCCIII.*

It should have been added, that, although Barnham speaks of 'the common sort of women', yet the ladies were scarcely more decent, at least not in England, as it is sufficiently proved by the passages quoted in my edition of Shakespeare's Tragedy of Hamlet (Halle, 1882), p. 192 seqq. and in my *Abhandlungen zu Shakespeare*, S. 405.

CCCIV.*

Sorrowful, in Antony and Cleopatra, I, 3, 64, and *widowhood*, in Milton's Samson Agonistes, 958, are used as dissyllables:—

With sor|r'wful wa|ter? Now | I see, | I see.
Cherish | thy hast|en'd wid'|whood with | the gold.
Compare also Prof. Skeat's Etymological Dictionary s. *Arrow*.

CCCVI.*

At page 175, l. 19 read: *A* COURSE *more prom'sing* instead of *A* CAUSE *more prom'sing*; *cause* being a misprint of the Globe Edition that has led both Mr Fleay (*apud* Ingleby l. l. p. 92) and myself into error.

The scansion of a line in The Winter's Tale (II, 3, 137) given at p. 178, had better be withdrawn, as I think it now far more probable that this line should be scanned:—

And by | good test|'mony, or | I'll seize | thy life.
The words *testimony* and *or* are to be run into one another,
and the connective (*And*) need not be omitted.

CCCIX.*

In two well-known German books I have discovered two
instances in point which go far to establish almost beyond
the reach of doubt the insertion of *fast* before *last* as suggested by me. The first instance occurs in Eichendorff's
celebrated novel '*Aus dem Leben eines Taugenichts*', Chap. IV,
at the beginning of the last paragraph but one. Of the five
different editions which I have been able to compare the
Editio princeps (Berlin, 1826, Vereinsbuchhandlung, p. 58),
the illustrated edition published by M. Simion (Berlin, 1842,
p. 59), and the second edition of the *Sämmtliche Werke* (1864,
Vol. III, p. 44) correctly read: *Was war mir aber das alles
(Alles) nütze, wenn ich meine lieben lustigen Herrn (Herren)
nicht wieder fand?* In the more recent editions, however,
which were published by Ernst Julius Günther (Leipzig, 1872,
p. 61) and by C. F. Amelang (Leipzig, 1882, p. 61) we read:
*Was mir aber das Alles nütze, wenn ich meine lieben lustigen
Herren nicht wiederfand?* In these editions *war* has dropped
out, no doubt from its similarity with the preceding *Was*,
from which it differs only by a single letter. Still more
striking is the second instance, which is taken from the
'*Jugenderinnerungen eines alten Mannes (Wilh. v. Kügelgen)*'
(Berlin, Hertz) of which I have looked up the second, fifth,
and ninth edition. In the second edition (Berlin, 1870) we
read at p. 31: *Nicht weniger befremdlich war es der Mutter,
dass Wetzel seine würdige Frau nie anders nannte als "Henne"*

*und sein niedliches Töchterchen "Forelle". Er dagegen behaup-
tete, unsere gewöhnlichen Taufnamen seien gar zu albern und
hätten nicht die geringste Bedeutung. Unter Amalie, Charlotte,
Louise, Franz und Balthasar, und wie die Leute alle hiessen,
könne sich kein Mensch was denken. Namen müssten das Ding
bezeichnen, gewissermassen abmalen, und wenn er seine Frau
"Henne" nenne, so hätte Jedermann damit ein treues Bild ihres
Wesens und ihrer Beschäftigungen, wie denn auch seine Tochter
eine veritable Forelle sei.'* In the fifth and ninth edition,
however, (p. 31 in either edition), the word *Henne* before
nenne has been omitted, evidently from no other cause than
from its similarity to it. The two words differ merely in
their initial letters (*H* and *n*), and in so far the case is
completely analogous to: *He held me fast last night* &c.
(See Kölbing, *Englische Studien*, VIII, 495).

THE END.